Heavy Traffic

Karen Goldner

Also by Karen Goldner

Passing Semis in the Rain

ISBN-10: 1983448052
ISBN-13: 978-1983448058

To Chicago, of course.

Prologue

Krista Jordan loved to drive. But living in the city, only a few "L" stops away from her office in Chicago's West Loop, she rarely drove, and didn't even own a car. For Krista, sailing down I-55 in rural Illinois was a rare treat, a break from the constant pressure of leading her growing technology company.

When she started Pro Traffic five years ago she had sold her car. Every penny counted, and she needed the cash more than she needed a late model hybrid. While the company had become profitable, Krista retained the frugal habits she had learned scraping by in the early days. Still, when business required her to travel, like it did tonight, she was more than happy to pick up a car share rental and hit the open road. Traffic was thinning the farther she drove past Chicago's congested South Suburbs, and the sky became pink from the fading sun.

Tomorrow was an important meeting with the City of Peoria. Krista had intended to spend some windshield time thinking about her strategy, but as rural Illinois's green fields whizzed by, she let her inventor's mind wander. She thought about how the creator of television had been inspired by the crisscrossed lines he had plowed as a farm boy. She, too, liked to play with patterns in her head. She found it relaxing, and often a way to break through problems.

It was such musing that had led Krista to develop a street light signalization system that was safer and more energy efficient than her competition. Pro Traffic had grown from nothing more than an idea into a successful startup with two dozen employees. Krista's focus and determination had made that happen. Her focus now should have been closing the Peoria sale, but she allowed herself to think about another, larger prize.

The City of Chicago contract. Nearly seven million people drove on streets that used her company's technology, from Seattle to Baltimore, but none of them were in her hometown. Since the beginning, Krista had been told it was fruitless to try to dislodge the incumbent contractor, Stendahl Technology. Everyone said so: aldermen, business colleagues, a couple of friends at City Hall. Stendahl had been Chicago's vendor so long that no one could remember when the first contract had been signed. But Krista didn't give up.

Finally they had found an alderman who would listen, with an aide who was willing to make some due diligence calls, checking how their system worked in other cities. The aide heard glowing reports, and shared those reports with the alderman. Word had spread among a small caucus, and a presentation had been scheduled for the end of June. Krista and her team had been working on the first draft of the presentation since before Memorial Day. They were close, and Krista allowed herself the luxury of imagining that meeting as darkness fell.

Her reverie was broken when her car jolted forward. For a moment she thought she'd run over something. The car jolted again. She'd been rear ended. Looking in the rearview mirror, she saw a car so close she could make out the shapes of two men in its front seat. She sped up. They hit her again, and this time they didn't back off. Their car pushed her onto the shoulder. Krista glanced around, panicked. She saw the headlights of northbound traffic across the median, and leaned on the horn, but the headlights continued forward, steady, giving no sign anyone noticed.

She accelerated and pulled back onto the road. The other car rammed her left rear fender, pushing Krista's vehicle off the shoulder down into a steep drainage swale. She accelerated again, trying unsuccessfully to steer her car up the uneven ground back onto the road. The car behind pushed into her fender again, just as her front tire hit a sharp rock and blew.

Krista screamed as her car bounced and tilted onto its right side. Another push from the car behind, and it flipped to the right, sliding down the wall of the swale. Its front bumper hit bottom after about ten feet. Her airbag deployed at the same time Krista's leg, hyperextended to reflexively stomp the brake pedal, snapped. She screamed again, this time from pain.

The car tottered on its side and Krista was suspended several feet above ground. She was held in place by the seatbelt, and pushed upright by the airbag. Her purse and cell phone had fallen out of reach, lying against the passenger door below her. She considered how to free herself without further injuring her broken leg, when a bright light appeared from behind her car. She heard voices. Her heart leapt at first: help—or were these the drivers from the car that ran her off the road? She struggled to unfasten the seatbelt.

"Hold on, we're gonna get the car right," said a man's voice. So it was help. Where had the drivers of the attack car gone?

"My leg is broken but I'm okay otherwise," Krista found herself saying. Her voice was stronger than she felt.

"Grab onto something," said the man.

The airbag blocked the steering wheel, so Krista held onto the door handle. Her car was pulled back to the left, bouncing as all four wheels were grounded. The pain in her leg was excruciating, made worse from the impact, but Krista breathed a sigh of relief.

A man tapped on the driver's side window. "You Krista Jordan?" he asked.

Her stomach clenched. How did he know her? These guys weren't help. She said nothing. Maybe someone on the road had heard her horn and called the state police. Maybe.

The man got louder. "You Krista Jordan?"

Another man, shorter than the first, appeared. "Open this door," he ordered Krista. And to his partner, "Check the floor for her purse."

The taller man disappeared.

"Who the hell are you?" Krista's response to fear was anger. "What are you doing?"

The tall man reappeared at the passenger window. Krista was surrounded. Her mind raced through her options. The horn had been disabled when the airbag deployed. She wouldn't be able to run on her broken leg, but if she could reach her cell phone, and drag herself to the road…

"Unlock the fucking door," yelled the shorter man, who continued to tug on the handle. Krista heard a sharp pounding noise on the passenger side, followed by the window breaking. She turned to see the passenger door open, the tall man grabbing her purse and cell phone from the floor.

Krista kept shouting for help as she reached around, trying to find something sharp. There was nothing within reach. The glove box was empty. She dug her fingers deep between the seat and the center console, hoping for a pen or a paper clip. Nothing. Her shouts began to fade, then adrenalin kicked in with shrieks of panic. She could smell her own sweat.

The man pulled out her driver's license and tilted it to catch the beam of light from his car. "That's her. That's the one."

"Bring the hammer over here," the man at her window said.

Krista's eyes filled with tears and her stomach churned. She thought about her parents, her brother, her nephews. Her on-again, off-again boyfriend. Her employees at Pro Traffic who had become like family. Why was this happening? It didn't make sense. She pulled at the door handle, desperately hoping she could rip it out and use it as a weapon.

The window next to her head shattered and a hand reached for the lock on the door console. Krista grabbed two of the man's thick fingers and pulled them apart. She heard him curse. She leaned in to bite his finger, but he hit her in the jaw when he recoiled his hand. The blow made her bite her tongue, and she wasn't sure whether the blood she tasted was his or her own.

"Bitch!" he howled.

The shorter man laughed. "Let me do it." He reached through the window and gripped Krista by the neck, holding her against the headrest. He protected the fingers of his other hand in a fist, thrusting it inside the car. Krista lunged at him but could do nothing more than scratch his arm as he quickly flipped the lock with his thumb. The car door opened. Krista waved her arms, frenzied to protect herself. The taller man grabbed her hair, pulling her head and shoulders out of the car. She screamed again, and tried to jerk away. Her head was unprotected. Looking up, from the light of the car behind she finally got a good look at one of the assailants: a stranger with dead eyes and pursed lips. He held a hammer above his head. She twisted again as he began to swing his arm downward, but she could not avoid its path.

"How much we gettin' for this?" Krista heard as the light vanished.

1

"Something's wrong," I said to Charlie. We sat in his office on the second floor of a nice enough building in a not too bad part of Miami. Charlie was behind his desk, which had probably looked contemporary and professional in the nineties, long before we met. I sat across from him in a green leatherette chair, selected as the guest seat in his office because it was the only one, besides his own, that wasn't cracked or covered with files. "It doesn't smell right. Why would they hire us?"

"Rule Number One of the security business." Charlie Mason peered at me over his laptop, which was perched precariously on top of a stack of files. "Never pass up a paying job."

"But why wouldn't they hire somebody from Chicago? There must be dozens of security firms up there. And for them not to tell you what we're protecting them from? That isn't a red flag?"

"Tina." Charlie shut his laptop and sighed. "They like us, they like you, and they don't trust anybody in Chicago. And they've paid for the first two weeks in advance. Expenses and all." I started to protest again and he raised his hand to stop me. "We're taking this job. Bill's already on his way, and your flight leaves tomorrow at ten. Go home and pack. Don't overthink this."

"I started to do a little checking."

The small curve of a smile on Charlie's face vanished into a tight line, and his cheeks reddened until they matched the color of his nose.

"You did what?"

"I did a little background investigating."

"On the client?" He stood up, hands gripping the edge of his desk, and he leaned toward me, his voice rising. "On the client?" I remained on my green leatherette perch and made a conscious decision to avoid shrinking from him. Part of me still wanted to retreat from hostile authority, and that part had to be reminded I was only here because I wanted to be.

"Yes," I said, managing to sound cool—at least, it sounded that way to me. "The client. The people who are flying us fourteen hundred miles to protect them but won't say from what. I thought that when things didn't feel right, we were supposed to trust our instincts."

Charlie dropped his voice and emphasized every syllable.

"You are not an investigator. You provide physical security to the people who pay us for that service. Those people pay me, and I pay you. You are paid to think on your feet to protect our clients, but you are not paid to investigate."

I stared back, refusing to react. I thought about my bank account, and must have smiled a little. This was a mistake: not sure how to take my expression, Charlie decided I was baiting him which simply added fuel to his rage.

"You think this is funny? You think you're above all this now? Don't confuse some online criminal justice class you've taken with knowing anything about investigative work. I brought you into this firm knowing nothing. Nothing. And now you repay me by screwing around playing Girl Detective?"

That was enough. I stood and began to walk toward the door.

"You're getting on that plane, right? Tina Johnson, do you like this job? You need this job."

He was right on the first two and wrong on the third. When we had met, I was unemployed and the money Charlie offered was more than I'd ever earned, or ever thought I could. Since then, my circumstances had taken a turn for the better. I kept working for Mason Security because I enjoyed it, and it seemed smart to let Charlie continue thinking I was the same middle-income middle-aged woman he had helped out just over a year ago. Having a lot of money can change relationships, and I had a feeling it would have changed ours for the worse. Still, I wasn't going to let him think he was forcing me into something.

I turned to him. "Yes, I'm taking the assignment. Out of curiosity more than anything. Plus I've never been to Chicago, and I hear it's beautiful in the summer."

2

Angela

Angela Frank had said good-bye to her boss, Krista, when Krista left for Peoria that evening. Angela left the office soon after, looking forward to enjoying a particularly beautiful June night. She walked to the Red Line "L" station and had been happily surprised to find a seat. Thirty minutes later she descended the stairs at the Bryn Mawr Avenue platform. Five minutes after that, she unlocked her apartment door. A noise came up behind her.

Lester.

"Hi, Angie." No one ever called her Angie except her octogenarian neighbor. When he said it, Angela always smiled.

"Hi, Lester." She turned to see him standing in his doorway across the hall, an even older-looking man behind him. "You've got company." Angela hoped this would let her off the hook. She liked Lester B. Moore, but it had been a long day.

"I do. And he knows you." Lester's eyes twinkled and his grin revealed most of his remaining teeth.

Angela peered around him for a closer look. Lester's guest was short and chubby. At one point, perhaps during the Eisenhower Administration, he would have been considered stocky, maybe even powerfully built. Now his most dominant feature was his nose. Angela didn't like to condemn a nose by calling it "bulbous," but she could think of no better word.

"I'm sorry," she said to the man, moving reluctantly toward Lester's door. "I don't remember when we met."

The man laughed. "Oh, we haven't. And believe you me, I'd remember meeting a girl as pretty as you. Such beautiful curly hair." Angela reflexively touched her long dark hair and smiled. With Lester as her neighbor, she was used to old men flirting, and she found it endearing.

She extended her hand.

"Well, it's a pleasure to meet you."

"Stuart Mackenzie, and the pleasure is all mine." He grinned broadly as he took her olive-toned hand in his beefy pale one. "Lester here was telling me about your grandmother. She worked at the Edgewater Hotel, right? So did I."

Angela's stomach growled. Lester heard it and laughed.

"Where are my manners? Stu and I were just about ready to have some cookies and beer. Come on in."

Angela's stomach would have been happier with a pizza, but an immediate cookie seemed better than waiting to heat up the frozen Connie's in her apartment. Besides, she was intrigued. She stepped into Lester's dusty apartment and accepted refreshments.

"You worked with Grandma Dot?" Angela asked as she began her second cookie. Lester liked to splurge on treats from the coffee shop around the corner.

Stu settled back in a chair that looked nearly as old as he was, ready to hold court. He cleared his throat and dramatically sipped his beer. Angela and Lester waited with appropriate respect.

"Well," Stu finally announced, "I worked at the Edgewater back in the thirties and forties, and Lester mentioned that your grandmother Dot did, too. Dot Bragg, right?"

Angela nodded. "That was her maiden name. She was a housekeeper until it closed."

"Nineteen sixty-seven. Sad ending." Stu shook his head over the memory and then brightened up. "But back in the day, it was *the* place in Chicago. D'ya know it was the only hotel like it, other than in Biloxi? Right on the beach, like a palace on the lake."

"Tell me about my grandmother. I was a little girl when she died, and she never told any stories about the Edgewater." Angela slipped her tired feet from her low-heeled shoes and curled them underneath her on the couch.

"Your grandmother was a sweet girl. Friendly, but quiet."

"Were you friends?"

"Dot mostly kept to herself. Most of the other maids were Irish, and they were a tight bunch. Dot was more a loner. I never understood that, her being so pretty and all. A couple of the other guys asked her out, but she seemed to have her eyes on…" Stu stopped. Perhaps he had said too much, especially to a granddaughter.

Despite his penchant for introducing himself as "Less Be More," a moniker he never ceased to find amusing, Lester B. Moore did not believe that one could say too much.

"Her eyes on who?" Les asked. "Some good-looking guest?" He winked at Angela. "Maybe one of those ballplayers who would hang out in the bar?"

Stu took a long swig of beer, his amnesia persisting. Angela's curiosity pushed the thought of Connie's pizza from her mind. She popped the tab on the sweating can that Les had set in front of her, took a drink, and sat back.

"I've heard that's where all the famous people stayed," she said. Maybe a slight detour would get the old man talking again.

Stu took the bait and began a monologue of tales from the Edgewater Beach Hotel that reminded Angela of a British serial. His stories were funny, all G-rated, and few of them involved Dot except as an onlooker. Angela had sipped half the beer when she tried to bring the conversation back to her grandmother.

"You made it sound like Grandma Dot had a boyfriend. Was it you?"

Stu's laugh rattled more like a cough. He was back to treading in dangerous waters. "No, not me."

"Then who? I'd like to know. I'd like to know what she was like. All I remember was that she made ham hocks and amazing peach cobbler, wore housedresses and kept her apartment neat as a pin, and always had hard candy in a bowl." Angela grinned. "I'd love to learn more about her as a young woman. Young women have boyfriends. It's okay. I'm curious."

Stu gave in.

"Well, Dot was a looker. Real nice girl, but she seemed a little lonely sometimes. She didn't have any family up here, at least none that she ever mentioned. She said she'd grown up on the South Side, but never said more than that." He took a long sip of beer. "There was this guy in the neighborhood named Larry DeLuca. Word was that he was some kind of cousin of Vince DeLuca."

"DeLuca? He was a pretty big mobster back in the day." Lester seemed satisfied at his contribution to the conversation, and walked into the kitchen.

"Larry wasn't bigtime or anything, but he was a little shady. Not the type of guy a girl's parents would have wanted her to bring home." Stu finished his beer. "But I liked him in a way. I never personally saw him do anything to anybody. He was a smart guy, funny, and friendly: he never met a stranger."

Lester returned with three more beers. Stu popped the last bite of cookie into his mouth and accepted a cold can from his friend. Angela smiled and shook her head "no." Lester placed a can on the coffee table in front of her anyway. She grabbed a cookie, still turned toward Stu. He took a gulp of the fresh beer and continued.

"Larry was good looking, no doubt. A sharp dresser and always had spending money. He sometimes came into the hotel for a drink, although the manager would chase him out if he saw him, on account of his cousin. He and Dot started to get a little sweet on each other. They were an odd couple, her being such a nice girl, and so shy."

"Opposites attract," intoned Lester wisely. Angela smiled, nodded, took another bite of cookie, and waited for the rest of the story.

"They went out and, well, that was in the days before there was a lot you could do about it and—" Stu took a breath, his eyes focused on the floor. "She got pregnant."

The men stared at anywhere but Angela, waiting for a reaction. All she could come up with was a question.

"When was this?"

"Forty-two. I left before the baby came; went into the Army. I heard from some buddies that Dot had a little girl, but she sent the baby to live with her sister or someone. That happened a lot back then."

Lester nodded solemnly in agreement.

"My mother was born in 1949. And her father, my grandfather, was Dominic Damico." Angela considered this a moment. "So I have an aunt?"

"I guess so. Do you want to hear the rest?" Stu asked. Lester shifted forward in his chair.

Angela was surprised there was more. "Of course."

"After I came home from Europe, in '45, I went back to the Edgewater. By then, Larry was in prison for robbing a bar in Uptown. Dot never talked about him, but then again, she never talked about much of anything personal. By the late forties—that's right, it was Christmas of '48, because that's when I started seeing my Lois—Larry was out. And Dot must have been waiting for him, because before you knew it they were back together."

"Did they get married?"

Stu swallowed a bite of cookie. "Your grandmother said they were going to. But then it happened." He swigged the last of his beer, raising his eyebrows dramatically.

"It?" Les and Angela asked in unison.

"That bar in Uptown? The one Larry had robbed while I was overseas? Well, a bartender at that same place was killed in 1949. Stabbed to death. The police said it was an attempted hold-up, and that Larry had done it."

"Had he?" The story took on a surreal quality to Angela. She popped open the second beer.

Stu shrugged. "That's what everybody said. He was the easy guy to pin it on, since he'd robbed it before. But nobody knew for sure. Larry took off before they could arrest him. Word was his cousin moved him down to Mexico, which seems likely." Stu shrugged again. "I don't know that anyone really knew where he went. A cop

13

friend of mine said the investigation ended when he disappeared, because everybody was so sure that it was him."

The three sat in silence until Lester couldn't hold it in anymore. "So who was Dominic Damico?"

"A nice kid from the neighborhood," Stu said. "Dom had a steady job, although now I don't remember doing what. He always had a crush on your grandmother from a ways off. He was a little older than she was, and ready for a family."

"He was my grandfather." Angela wasn't sure whether she was making a statement or asking a question.

Stu shrugged. "Maybe. The word was that Dot and Larry were getting married because they had to. I got married myself in February of '49, and we moved out to Park Forest, so I didn't see Dot after that. Never knew for sure if she was in the family way or not, but when I heard later that she married Dom, I assumed that he rescued Dot from having to give up another baby."

"Wow." Now it was Angela's turn to look at the floor. The two men waited for her to say something more. "Wow. That's quite a...a thing. I don't know what to say."

"Maybe I shouldn't have told you." Stu's forehead wrinkled.

"No, I'm glad you did," Angela said, and she meant it. "It's a lot to digest. I don't think my mother knows. She would have told me if she knew." She realized that she was wringing her hands together and stopped, spreading them out on her lap. Then she brightened. "My dad's an only child, too, so I didn't have any aunts or uncles. I always wanted one."

Stu and Lester nodded at her anxiously. Angela stared at her hands in her lap, then looked at the two old men. Their faces were full of concern, and she felt an obligation to smile at them.

"I wonder what my mom is going to say. She has a sister, somewhere." Angela swung her feet to the floor and reached for her shoes. "I wonder whether I could find her."

"The first step would be to track down the Braggs. I'll bet they have old city directories at the History Museum." Stu's forehead smoothed and his eyes brightened at the thought of detective work.

"Stu Mackenzie, this isn't your business," Lester interjected, his concern for Angie powerful enough to overtake his curiosity.

Stu looked chastened. "You're right. But if you want any help, I'm happy to oblige."

Angela stood up, still not sure what she was feeling.

"Stu, it was nice to meet you. Thanks for telling me this. I think." She tried another smile, and let herself out before Stu and Lester could get out of their chairs.

3

Cousin Tom

Whenever his uncle came into the office, Thomas Donnelly's stomach turned into knots tighter than the ones his construction crews used to control steel girders.

"Uncle Floyd, how are you?"

"Tom, you shouldn't ask a question when you don't care about the answer. I'm here to look over the files on the Ashland project."

If the Ashland project had been particularly large or important or difficult, Tom wouldn't have minded his uncle's intrusion. It was Floyd's company, after all. But Floyd Stendahl's interest in the Ashland job, or the little building on Elston last week, or the thoroughly routine renovation of a commercial office on North Avenue the week before, was simply a way of making sure that Tom understood the limits of his own competence and authority in managing the construction division of the Stendahl Group.

So Tom sighed to himself and turned on the computer at the intern's desk, opening the file for his boss. Floyd poured the last of the coffee into a cup bearing the name of a long failed bank.

An insensitive man might not have noticed that Floyd seemed more flustered than usual when he sat down at the computer, and an unkind man might have taken some delight in it. Tom was neither, so he observed his uncle curiously for a few minutes while Floyd nervously scanned files that were in perfect order.

"Everything okay?" Tom asked. "Did you want to look at anything else?"

"No, no, everything looks fine. Nice job."

Nice job? Now Tom knew something was wrong. He had brewed another pot of coffee, and without needing to ask, refilled Floyd's cup along with his own.

"What's the matter, Uncle Floyd? You seem preoccupied."

Tom's mother, Floyd's baby sister, had suffered through half a decade of Alzheimer's before her death and Tom was constantly on alert for signs in his uncle.

"What?" Floyd asked absently. He took the coffee and looked at Tom. "Everything is fine here. I'm just a little concerned about the city contract."

The Stendahl Group comprised multiple divisions with annual revenue of over a billion dollars. It employed one thousand two hundred twenty-one people and had multi-million-dollar customers around the globe, most of them units of government. Still, when Floyd said "the city contract," Tom knew exactly what he meant. The knots pulled tighter.

"Is there a problem with the renewal?"

"Maybe. It's not for another eight months, but I'm hearing noises I don't like from a couple of the aldermen. I've had Bob taking some steps to protect it, but I don't know whether we've done enough."

This was not an answer that made Tom feel better. His cousin, Bob, was president of the Stendahl Group—at least, when Floyd allowed him to function that way. In college, Bob Stendahl had taken *some steps* with a couple of fraternity brothers to pass an exam. Those steps had earned Bob a disciplinary action that only the timely gift of an endowed chairmanship erased. Tom had learned never to ask a Stendahl for details about *some steps*. And that wasn't Tom's role in the business, anyway. He limited his involvement with the City of Chicago to filing straightforward building plans and pulling straightforward construction permits. He left the messier parts to Bob and Floyd.

So Tom sipped his coffee quietly and sympathetically and waited for Floyd to remember their division of labor. Floyd did, and closed up the harmless Ashland files. He thanked his nephew for the coffee, but did not say goodbye when he left.

4

"Has anyone heard from Krista? I wonder how the Peoria meeting went."

Angela looked up from her laptop. The question came from Denise, Pro Traffic's admin/human resources manager, but Angela herself was equally curious about how the morning meeting had gone. It would have ended hours earlier, but internal communication was not Krista Jordan's strong suit. She was a techie whose skills were most appreciated by other technical people. She could close a deal by virtue of her engineering knowledge and the sheer force of her will, but it was not uncommon for her to forget to keep her employees informed.

"I can't get her on her cell," Denise said. "I've texted and emailed. Nothing."

Angela joined her coworkers in confirming that no, Krista had not been in touch.

Denise shook her head.

After three years of working for Krista, Angela was used to her boss's communication lapses, and her concentration returned to her laptop. She had spent the morning distracted, thinking about Stu's news, and was now making up for lost time on the presentation for a prospect that would make the Peoria contract seem like a beta test site: Chicago.

Angela had met Krista through mutual friends three years before. Krista's determination and vision were a dramatic change from the malaise Angela was experiencing in her corporate marketing job. She traded security for the wild ride of a startup, and had never looked back.

The two women were well suited to work together, with Angela having a sense for business that Krista, the engineer, sometimes lacked. They'd been together through the highs and lows of finding investors and making their initial sales. Angela still viewed Krista with a sense of awe, and never ceased to be amazed at her boss's technical brilliance and dedication. It wasn't difficult for Angela to understand and accept Krista's few limitations.

Now she was nearly done with the presentation; all that was lacking were a couple of pieces of information from Krista. Angela looked at her watch: five thirty. She would probably hear from Krista later in the evening and could finish it at home. In the meantime, it was another gorgeous evening and she could use a run.

The Lake Shore Trail was busy with runners, bikers, and walkers as Angela set out south from Bryn Mawr. She occasionally glanced at Lake Michigan, dotted with white sails. Early-season beachgoers spread their towels on Foster Beach. She dodged a woman pushing a stroller and thought about her genealogical research, not twenty-four hours old.

After her conversation with Stu and Lester, Angela had immediately called her mother. Joyce Damico Frank would hear none of it. Stu—"that old man," she had called him—was simply wrong. He had gotten Dot Bragg—"my mother!"— confused with another girl, or was retelling gossip that had been a lie seventy years ago, or was drunk, or simply malicious.

Angela had finally dropped the topic. Her mother's conviction caused her some doubts about a stranger's tale, and without evidence it was nothing but a tale. Still, she couldn't shake the story from her mind. She had stayed up late exploring online, arriving at a list of Braggs who lived in Chicago in 1942.

There were ninety-five. She was overwhelmed at first: a list over sixty years old of nearly one hundred possible Braggs. Even that list was inadequate, Angela had thought, as Dot's sister was probably married when she took the baby, Angela's alleged aunt. There was no way to know her married name. Angela was searching for Dot's parents, her own great grandparents, who were surely long dead.

She had turned the problem over and over in her head as she herself rolled over and over in bed, unable to fall asleep. After an hour, she realized she had a resource in Justin, who at twenty-nine was Pro Traffic's senior developer. If anyone could figure out what to do with her list, Justin could. That relaxed her mind enough to finally fall asleep.

In the morning—at least late in the morning, when Justin and the other developers started wandering in to work—she had brewed him a double espresso and approached with a smile.

"Justin, I've got a puzzle."

He took the white ceramic cup from her. His clean-shaven face was pale as usual under his scraggly brown hair, and adorned with large horn-rimmed glasses.

"A puzzle? What kind?"

"A database puzzle, I guess you'd say. I'm trying to track down a person born in 1942 by the name of Bragg. I've got a list of ninety-five Braggs who lived in Chicago that year. I'm not sure which one is correct."

"And by 'correct,' you mean the person who was born in 1942?"

"Yes, or at least their family." Angela had been pleased to see Justin squint with interest through his horn rims.

"What is the person's name?"

"I don't know. She's a woman."

"No name? That makes it harder. Where are these Braggs?"

"In Chicago."

"It's a good thing for you that I like puzzles." He had drained the double espresso and set the cup on his IKEA glass-topped desk, turning to his computer with relish.

Now, as she turned back at Irving Park Road, her two-mile mark, Angela smiled with anticipation. Justin had spent an hour on the project before having to get down to Pro Traffic work. He told her he would get back to it this evening.

She ran north and wondered about Krista. Although it wasn't surprising for Krista to forget to keep her employees informed of minutiae, the Chicago presentation was important. Angela had expected to hear from her boss by now. She glanced at her phone: nothing.

Angela reached Bryn Mawr Avenue and was walking from the Lake Shore Trail to her apartment when she ran into Stu, leaning against the red brick wall of the coffee shop.

"Waiting for Lester?" she joked.

Stu looked uncomfortable to see her. "Maybe I shouldn't have said what I did last night," he said. "Your grandmother was a really nice girl."

Angela was both amused and touched by his old-fashioned propriety. "But it's true, right? I've started trying to track down her family to see if I can find my aunt."

Stu's fuzzy white eyebrows went up and he broke into a relieved grin. "That's my girl. And of course it's true. One thing that Stuart Mackenzie is *not* is a liar. If I can be of assistance, let me know. Lester knows how to get me. I live in Uptown, but this place has a half-price senior citizen special, so I'm up here quite a bit. Good to get a little exercise, and cookies to boot."

A strong wind blew off the lake down Bryn Mawr. Angela started to feel a chill; it wasn't fully summer yet.

"I've got a friend helping me. I found nearly one hundred Braggs in the old city directory."

Stu attempted a suggestive smile and his eyebrows rose again. "A friend, eh? What kind of friend does a pretty girl like you have?"

Angela laughed. "You're terrible!" she teased back. "Not that kind of friend. He's a computer geek. I work with him."

"So there's still a chance for me?" Stu chortled.

Angela shook her head and smiled. "Sorry. Lester's ahead of you in line." She exaggerated a shrug.

The briefest look of disappointment crossed Stu's face as he remembered he was no longer thirty. "Lester's a lucky man," he joked.

"He's a good neighbor," Angela said. Her smile faded as she shivered. "I'm getting a little chilly from the wind. I'll keep Lester up to date on the search and will definitely let you know if I need your help."

Stu went into the coffee shop as Angela turned off Bryn Mawr and jogged down the block to her apartment building. Her one-bedroom unit was on the second story of a four-story building that had been recently renovated to combine the exterior charm of 1920s yellow terra cotta with all the modern conveniences twelve hundred dollars a month would buy. There was even an elevator, which was quite a luxury in a low-rise building, but most of the time Angela took the back stairs.

She slipped into her apartment, grateful for no sign of Lester, and took a hot shower.

Her email included nothing from Krista or Justin, so after making salad by dumping lettuce into a bowl and chopping up a tomato, she turned back to her Bragg search.

"Old school," she said to herself as she dug a fold-out map of Chicago from the back of a drawer. The map was so old that she couldn't remember where she got it or why. Now it would come in handy. She moved her laptop out of the way and spread the map on her desk. Using the paper copy of her list, she began to plot the addresses.

She found Dot Bragg, with an address on Berwyn. It was only a few blocks away from Angela's apartment, just down the street from where the hotel had been, and near the Berwyn "L" station. Angela smiled as she remembered visiting her grandmother's walk-up as a child. Part of what had attracted her to the Edgewater neighborhood, along with rents that had once been affordable, was that memory.

Angela returned to the map. Her strategy was to look for a cluster of Braggs, hoping that if there were several in one area, someone in that neighborhood might possibly remember the family. A long shot, but she didn't know what else to do while she waited for Justin to work his digital magic.

Chicago's grid system made most of the addresses easy to find. A number of them were in places that were no longer residential, having been replaced by shopping centers or universities. Dead ends. Some were on the West Side, which she discounted based on Stu's recollection of Grandma Dot's family being from the South Side.

Many addresses were on South Park Way, a street that was not on her map. Finally she checked online and learned South Park Way had been renamed Martin Luther King Jr. Drive in 1968. A few of the addresses were now part of the Illinois Institute of Technology between 31st and 35th Streets. In all, a large cluster of Braggs had lived in the neighborhood south and east of the expressways.

Bronzeville.

Angela had always thought that Bronzeville was predominately African-American, but decided there must have been a few white families. Or maybe Stu's recollection was off and Grandma Dot's sister lived elsewhere.

She was starting to think about what to do with the map when her phone rang. She looked at the number as she answered.

"Justin, have you found anything?"

"Yes. I found her. Your aunt's name is Linda Patterson."

5

"You found her? How?" Angela turned from the map and looked out her window, staring at the tree across the street without seeing anything.

"An Illinois adoption database," Justin said. He spoke slightly faster and higher than his normal flat tone. "She had registered as looking for her mother. It wasn't hard."

"That is amazing, Justin." Angela had worked with him long enough to know that when Justin said something wasn't hard, he was building up to something big.

"Do you want her phone number?"

"Her phone number? Of course! Does she live in Chicago? How many Linda Pattersons must there be?"

"Finding her name wasn't hard, but hacking into the registry to get her contact information was a little harder."

Angela grinned at the pride in Justin's voice.

"Thank you so much." She sat down and grabbed a pen and a pad of paper. "What can I do to repay you?"

Justin guffawed at the thought of something he knew he shouldn't say. Angela rolled her eyes and shook her head with a half smile.

"You can buy me lunch sometime," he finally said.

"That is a deal," said Angela. She wrote Linda Patterson's phone number on a white square of paper and hung up, butterflies taking over her stomach. She looked at the numer for a long time, then at the clock. It was nearly eight thirty. Not too late to call, right? At eight thirty-two, she dialed. A woman answered.

"Hello?"

"Is this Linda Patterson?"

"May I ask who's calling?" The woman's voice had the formality of someone whose profession had included a lot of phone calls.

"My name is Angela Frank. I'm trying to reach the Linda Patterson who was born at Edgewater Hospital in 1942." Angela took a breath. "She...she may be my aunt."

There was a pause so long that Angela thought she'd lost the call. As she was going to say something, the woman spoke.

"This is Linda Patterson. You have no idea how long I've wondered if I'd ever get this call."

Angela teared up, and the sniffle on the other end of the phone confirmed that her Aunt Linda was crying, too.

"I think that you and my mother are sisters."

"A sister?"

"Yes. Her name is Joyce Frank. Joyce Damico Frank. Her parents were Dot and Dominic Damico. At least, that's who we thought were her parents. It's possible that Dominic wasn't..." Angela realized how much she was saying, and how fast. She stopped talking.

"I knew Dot Damico. She's my mother's sister. I met her when I was a little girl." Another long pause. "Are you saying Dot Damico was my mother? How do you know? How did you find me?"

"This is a lot," Angela said. "I think maybe it might be better in person. Can we meet for coffee sometime soon?"

6

Mason Security had set me up with a hotel room on the Magnificent Mile. It was a beautiful June afternoon and only about a mile from the offices of our client, so I walked through the crowds of summer tourists rather than taking a cab.

Despite my misgivings about the reason I was in Chicago, I found myself swept up in the festive atmosphere. The flowers along Michigan Avenue were yellow and pink and purple and red. I let myself pretend I was on vacation for a few minutes and took a slight detour to see the Bean, the giant metal sculpture that reflects the skyline and spectators in every direction. Just before I reached the bronze lions that protect the Art Institute, I headed west on Monroe. Back to work.

My phone buzzed. It was a text from Teresa Traecy.

"Transferred funds as discussed." Teresa was my best friend and had become my financial manager. She was a banker with a terrific knack for picking investments. This was a skill that had become particularly valuable since she and I became millionaires the previous summer.

"Thanks," I typed, then added, "Wish you were here." I turned back to face Michigan Avenue and snapped a picture of the Art Institute. Not a postcard shot, but it would do. I pushed Send and thought about the unlikely circumstances of our friendship.

Teresa and I had met while I was on my way to New Orleans to escape from winter weather in Omaha and a life that had fallen apart. She was almost fifty, same as me, and we ended up solving a bank fraud in Miami and the attempted assassination of the President of Peru. During that unexpected series of events I had met Charlie Mason, who gave me a job when I needed one. A few months later, something even more unexpected happened: I received a reward from the government of a bit over a million dollars—for allowing them to recover funds in the bank fraud, not for saving a person's life, which I always thought was symptomatic of what was wrong with our country's priorities. However, I didn't send the money back. Teresa had returned to her home in Arkansas and she got a check, too. A million dollars was a lot of money, especially since I'd never had more than a few bucks squirreled away, but as I started doing the math I realized that it was a good idea to keep my job. I didn't tell Charlie or anybody at work about the money because it was easier that way. Teresa managed the funds well, and we'd seen an increase of nearly twenty percent in the last year.

I was so deep in thought that I almost missed my destination. The massive tower was made of glass and steel and stone, and our client's name was one of several engraved in bold letters on a large brass plate on an immense column in front of an imposing entryway. I hoped for a reflection from the revolving door to get a glimpse of my face and make sure I didn't have anything in my teeth, but all I could see was my brown hair, almost touching my shoulders, as I pushed through.

The building security guard, seated behind a low counter, confirmed my name on a list and pointed around the corner to a bank of elevators.

"Twenty-one," she said, turning her attention to two young and very handsome men in dark suits. I looked at my own black pantsuit. Charlie was particular about the type of clothing we wore, and my wardrobe now included more black pantsuits than I would have thought possible back when I was a telemarketer.

The elevator dinged at twenty-one, and I stepped into a lobby that was so white and well lit, it glowed. The lounge furniture, also white, looked expensive and uncomfortable. My eyes had barely adjusted to the bright light when a young woman's voice greeted me.

"Welcome to the Stendahl Group. May I help you?"

7

By the third day after Krista had gone missing, the Pro Traffic office was showing signs of wear. Denise was approaching frantic. Angela had stopped being able to come up with convincing or even plausible explanations for Krista's continued absence. Even the rest of the employees, all software engineers of one type or another and not prone to displays of emotion, looked worried.

They had learned that no, Krista had not arrived for the meeting in Peoria. No, she had not checked into the hotel in Peoria. Denise had ruminated for a full afternoon about whether to call Krista's brother in Ohio and decided that might panic the family, so she called Krista's sometime boyfriend instead. No, he had not heard from her. One of the programmers stopped by her condo twice. There had been no sign she was home and two restaurant flyers were sticking out from under her front door.

Finally Denise decided it was her job as Pro Traffic's HR manager to file a missing persons report. She felt that it needed to be done in person, so she Ubered to the police station. She'd been gone for over an hour when the office phone rang. As the only other person at Pro Traffic who did not constantly wear earbuds while staring at a laptop, Angela heard it, and picked up.

"Ms. Jordan rented a car from me on Monday. I've been unable to reach her," chastised a female voice with an Eastern European accent. "Do you know the whereabouts of the vehicle?"

"No," said Angela. "No one has heard from her. We're actually filing a police report now."

"Police report?" The woman's tone turned nervous. "Why a police report?"

"Because no one has seen her." Angela did not think she'd been unclear but slowed down just in case. "We've looked for her in all the places we can think of, and she has simply disappeared."

"With my car?" The voice returned to disapproval, and a slight rise of concern. For the car, not for Krista.

"I don't know," said Angela. "If there had been an accident, wouldn't the police notify you? They'd know that the car was registered to you, right?" This had been the conclusion reached at Pro Traffic; the lack of contact from the car share owner was seen as evidence that Krista had not been killed in a wreck.

"Yes, of course," the woman answered, too quickly.

"And then wouldn't you at least call us?"

"Yes, of course." A pause. "You are filing a report with the police?"

This woman is jumpy, thought Angela. Then again, she was a little jumpy, too. Angela wrote down the phone number from the caller ID. "Yes. What's your name so we can let you know what's going on with your car?"

The woman gave a remotely plausible name—too few syllables for someone with an Eastern European accent, thought Angela, but perhaps she was married. The whole thing was odd. The fact that it had taken this woman three days to call struck Angela as especially so.

Her cell was ringing: Denise. Reflexively she asked the woman for her phone number. The answer was not the same number on the caller ID but as she realized that the woman hung up.

"Are you in the office?" Denise's voice was even higher than it had been the past couple of days.

"Yes, right where you left me an hour ago. Are you at the police station? We just got a call from the place where Krista rented her car. They haven't seen her, either." There was a long pause before Denise spoke.

"Look, I need you to come over here. The police station at State and 18th. Don't tell anyone else right now, until we know for sure what's going on."

"What? Do they know where she is?" Angela was not reassured by Denise's tone.

"There's a chance that they know, and it's bad."

Angela grabbed her purse and the paper on which she had written both phone numbers and ran down Clinton until she could find a cab. When she arrived the station, Denise was inside, talking with a uniformed officer who was standing behind a counter that stretched the length of the cold, modern lobby. As Angela entered, Denise grabbed her in a bear hug and started to cry. The large waiting area held five or six people, none of whom paid the women any attention.

"They think she might be dead," Denise sobbed. "And that she stole a car."

"How could that be? Stole a car? No way." Angela pulled back and turned them both toward the officer.

"There was an incident," the officer said. His voice was calm and professional, but not warm. "On I-55 in Livingston County, downstate. The State Police found the car off the road. There had been a fatality, but there was no ID in the vehicle, so it was not possible to know the driver's identity right away. The car had been reported stolen a week ago."

"What happened? How do you know it's Krista?"

The officer ignored her questions. "Why would Ms. Jordan have been driving a stolen car?"

"I told her there is no way Krista would have stolen a car." Denise was nearly wailing.

"No, there's not," Angela agreed, keeping an even voice as she directed her comments toward the officer. "She rented a car to drive to Peoria for a meeting. She didn't show up at the meeting. She didn't check into the hotel. No one can figure out where she is. That's why Denise came to file a missing persons report." She remembered the note in her purse and pulled it out. "Just a few minutes ago we got a call from the car share person Krista was renting from. They hadn't been notified of any accident. If they reported that she stole the car, they had to be lying. Krista is a CEO, not a car thief."

The officer's expression remained deadpan but there was a flash of something in his eyes, like he was connecting dots that Angela was unaware of. The officer pointed them to a corner of the lobby and told them to wait. Fifteen minutes later, a heavy white man and a heavier black man, both wearing dark gray pants and white dress shirts, both of an indeterminate age north of forty, ushered them into a room not unlike the ones Angela had seen on TV crime shows.

When the four of them were seated at a gunmetal gray table, the black detective looked sympathetically at the women and opened a manila folder. He slid a photograph toward Denise and Angela. The face in the picture was severely damaged. Angela gasped and Denise averted her eyes.

"Is it Ms. Jordan?" asked the white detective.

Angela closed her eyes and nodded slowly. Denise dug into her purse for a tissue and came back empty-handed.

"I'm sorry, but we needed to make sure," the black detective said. Denise started to sob. He stepped out and returned with a box of tissue.

"Tell us about this phone call," instructed the white detective.

After telling the story from the beginning, and being asked questions that seemed design to trip them up should they have not been telling the truth, Angela finally was able to ask a question of her own: "What happened?"

"The car was off the road, crashed into a drainage ditch," answered the black detective. "It apparently happened after dark, so no one saw the car until the morning. It just looked like a typical late night accident—someone falling asleep at the wheel—but the fact that the driver had no identification struck the State Police as odd. Of course, the lack of ID also made the investigation harder. The medical examiner said there were head injuries inconsistent with a car crash, like she was hit with a blunt object. Plus, there was damage to the back of the car which initially wasn't considered because it could have been caused much earlier. Of course, with all this together we're considering it a possible homicide. Without ID, the victim could have been anyone, so they've circulated her description to local law enforcement to match against missing persons."

"And when they checked the registration that was when they learned the car was stolen?" Angela asked.

The detectives nodded.

"So you think it was stolen by the car share people? Like they stole a car and then rented it out? Is this something that's been a problem before?"

The black detective was a little more poker-faced than the white one, but that was clearly what they thought.

Denise pulled a tissue away from her nose long enough to ask, "Why? Who would do this to her?"

"That's what we want to find out, ma'am," said the black detective. Angela grabbed two more tissues from the box for Denise, then a third one for herself.

It was a long ride back to the office.

8

Angela did nothing Friday night but drink the bottle of wine she bought on her way home, finish off another one she found in the refrigerator, and call a friend who was suitably sympathetic. At least, she thought the friend had been sympathetic, but by Saturday she remembered only the hazy outlines of the conversation. Her head hurt and her stomach was threatening to rebel. She lay in bed, wishing she could levitate a glass of water to herself, when there was a knock at the door.

"Are you home? Stu's over and we're going to have cookies and beer."

Angela groaned. Her stomach nearly erupted as she staggered to the door. "Beer? What time is it?" She glanced at the kitchen clock as she asked. The answer was nearly one o'clock.

"I'm not dressed," she protested. "And I'm not feeling great today. Maybe a rain check?"

She knew as she said it that Lester would prevail. And he did, although she could claim a minor victory by forcing him to wait fifteen minutes while she attempted to make herself presentable. She was able to tie her hair back, but efforts to cool her swollen red eyes with a wet cloth were fruitless.

Lester laughed when he saw her at his door. He went into his kitchen, returning with tomato juice and ibuprofen.

"Did you find her?" Stu asked eagerly as they sat down in Lester's living room. Both men were grinning, which confused Angela. How could they be smiling about something as awful as Krista's death? Then she realized that wasn't who Stu meant.

"Yes, I found my aunt, but something else happened. Something bad. My boss was killed."

"Your boss?" Lester looked as shaken as Angela's stomach felt.

Stu stared at Angela, then at the can of beer in his hand.

Angela nodded. She didn't want to cry, and she knew that if she said anything the tears would flow. Instead, she gingerly sipped tomato juice.

"Sweetheart, I'm so sorry," Lester said. He leaned forward in his chair and reached his hand to her, patting her knee nervously.

Angela placed her hand on top of his and squeezed it. She smiled gratefully at him and nodded again.

"What happened?" Stu couldn't help himself.

"Let the poor girl sit for a minute," Lester scolded. To Angela he asked, "Can I get you anything?"

Angela shook her head "no" and stared at the tomato juice.

Lester retrieved his hand. He and Stu sat helplessly.

"I'm sorry," Angela said as she finally broke into tears. "I found out yesterday. My boss has been missing all week. She was driven off the road on her way to Peoria."

Stu watched as Lester handed Angela a box of tissue. They stared at the floor while she sobbed. Both men were surprised when, after a few minutes, she made a sound like a small laugh.

"I can't cry anymore," Angela said. "I'm too hungover. It hurts."

"You poor thing," said Lester, thankful for the reprieve. "How much did you drink?"

"I'm not sure." Angela tried to laugh at herself, but decided the safest course was to avoid any movement involving her stomach. "I think most of two bottles."

"Just keep working on that tomato juice," Stu counseled. "That does it for me every time."

Angela obeyed. She finished about a third of the glass.

"Not too fast," said Lester. "Slow and steady."

The three of them sat there a few minutes, all attention on the tomato juice. As Angela reached its halfway point, she took the ibuprofen with a swig. Then she set the glass down and leaned back, eyes closed.

"Are you okay?" Lester asked.

"Yes. I'm okay. I think I just need to go back to bed."

"But you said you found her. You found your aunt. Can't you tell us?"

Angela opened her eyes in time to see Stu receive a disapproving glance from Lester. She smiled at the men's silent bickering.

"Yes, of course. Her name is Linda Patterson. She lives in the South Loop and I spoke with her the night before last. She was excited to hear from me, I think."

"Have you met her yet?"

"No. She's coming over…wait, today is Saturday, right?"

"Yes," Stu and Lester answered in unison.

"She's coming over at two. I should have called her yesterday to postpone but I forgot."

"Honey, I'm sure that she'd understand."

"She's going to bring me a box of letters from Grandma Dot. She had thought Dot was her aunt…" Angela's voice trailed off. She looked at the clock, showing one-thirty, and was unable to conceive of a plan for either meeting Linda or cancelling. "She's probably already on her way. What is she going to think of me like this?" The tears returned.

Now it was Stu's turn to console. "Angie, of course she'll understand. Should we call her?"

Angela shook her head "no," miserable. "It's too late. I'll just go home and pull myself together. I do feel a little better," she offered. "Thank you for the juice."

Lester helped her up and walked her to the door, his hand on her elbow, and watched as she made it across the hallway. He shook his head sadly as she stepped into her apartment and shut the door. "Poor girl," he said to Stu, who nodded wisely in agreement.

Despite having said it was too late to cancel, Angela considered it one last time. A nap was just what she needed. But her first response had been correct: it was too late. Angela didn't want to be rude the first time she met her aunt.

She decided to change into something nicer than the jeans and T-shirt she'd managed for Lester and Stu. Her favorite beige capris were clean, which she took as a good sign. Even better, her headache had begun to ease. She was reapplying eye makeup and feeling nearly human when there was a knock at the door. The sound made her realize she hadn't put coffee on.

"Coming!" she called, scrambling to finish.

"No rush, dear. I'm early."

"Let me help you with that," said a male voice in the hallway. Stu. Angela shook her head, annoyed at his intrusion. She tried to think of a gentle way to shoo him away as she opened the door.

Once she saw the woman, she stopped thinking about Stu.

Linda Patterson was an inch or two shorter than Angela. She wore red slacks, a red and white polka dot blouse, and wire-rimmed glasses. But those were details that Angela wouldn't notice for a few seconds. What she saw immediately was the warm caramel color of the woman's skin.

Linda looked as confused as Angela.

"Angela Frank?"

"Yes, I am. You're Linda Patterson? I must have gotten the wrong person." Behind the woman, Lester had pushed his way into the hall and was standing next to Stu, who was holding a cardboard box. The men were wide eyed and silent.

"I am Linda Patterson." She paused and tilted her head slightly. With a single nod of understanding, a grin spread over her light brown face. "Honey, this explains everything."

Angela was still perplexed, although she found Linda's smile reassuring.

"Please, come inside." She held the door open for the older woman. Stu tried to enter her apartment, carrying the box. His face sank as Angela took it from him. "Stu, thank you, but I can get this now. See you guys later."

"If you need anything, we're right next door," Lester offered, not giving up his position in the hallway.

"I'm sure we'll be fine, but thank you." Angela moved into her apartment, balancing the box while pulling the door closed behind her with her foot. "Sorry about them," she said to Linda as she looked around for a place to set the heavy carton. "Stu, the guy in the hall, is a friend of my neighbor. He's the one who told me about you. Well, not you, exactly, but he is the one who told me my mom had a sister."

"Then I guess we owe him a debt of gratitude. I've been waiting a long time for this."

"Can I get you some coffee? I could use some, myself." Angela didn't wait for an answer before retrieving the filters from a cupboard.

"That would be nice, thank you." Linda stood at one end of Angela's galley kitchen. She waited until Angela had poured a pot of water into the coffeemaker. "I probably wasn't what you expected."

Angela turned toward Linda and smiled, shaking her head. "No, you weren't. And I'm guessing I don't look like the niece you thought you had?"

Linda laughed as the women moved through the open end of the kitchen.

"This is a lovely place." Linda sat on one of the two overstuffed chairs which, along with a love seat and a coffee table, comprised Angela's living room.

"Thanks. It's taken a while to replace the college furniture with real furniture, but it's almost the way I want it." Angela sat in the other chair. She resisted the urge to lean back; although she felt better than when she had awakened, the hangover was not quite done with her. She asked the obvious question. "You said 'this explains everything.' What did you mean?"

Linda looked at her hands, clasped in her lap. "I always had a sense that I was adopted. It was just a feeling, and I can't completely explain it. I didn't look like my father at all. Although they loved children, my parents never had any kids besides me. But they were great parents, and I didn't want to hurt them by asking about it, so I never did." Linda looked out the window. For a moment the only sound was the gurgling of the coffee maker. "Aunt Dot came to visit every so often when I was little. She had this sad look in her eye, and when she would leave, she'd hug me so tight." Linda closed her eyes for a moment. They were damp when she opened them. "I asked Mama why we never visited Aunt Dot at her house, why she always came to see us. Mama said that Aunt Dot lived too far away for us to visit. That didn't make sense to me, even then, although when you're a child you accept the world as your parents describe it."

The inviting aroma of coffee filled the apartment, but Angela didn't want to interrupt Linda's story.

"Aunt Dot brought a baby over once. At least, just one time that I can remember. I was in first grade, I think, or maybe second. The baby must have been your mother." Linda started crying as she spoke the words.

"I'm sorry to hit you out of the blue like this," Angela said, handing her a box of tissues.

"I think we're both being hit out of the blue," Linda said. She pulled three tissues out of the box and dabbed her eyes with one. "Aunt Dot was very light skinned. I thought she was white, but Mama told me that sometimes black people have light skin." She blew her nose and looked up at Angela. "Have you talked with your mother?"

"Yes," Angela said. "She didn't believe it at first, but after I told her I'd talked with you on the phone she said like you did, she said that things made more sense. But I'm not sure what she meant." She walked into the kitchen and called back, "Do you take anything in your coffee? I have milk and sugar."

"Milk, please," Linda said. She followed Angela and accepted a mug. The women stood at the counter, sipping and thinking.

"Mom wants to meet you, of course. She lives up in Evanston. Maybe we could all have dinner soon?"

Linda smiled. "I would love to. Tell me all about my sister."

The women spent the next hour introducing each other to their newly found families. Angela talked about losing Krista, and Aunt Linda held her close when she cried. After a few moments, Linda chuckled uncomfortably.

"What's wrong?" asked Angela.

"Honey, I feel bad, because I've always wanted to have a girl I could take care of. So here I am hugging you as you mourn your friend, and part of me is happy."

Angela sniffled and smiled. "I've always wanted to have an aunt, and I'm glad you're here."

They turned to examining the contents of the box. Linda said that her adoptive mother never threw correspondence away, and it showed. There were dozens of letters dating back seventy years. Some were from Dot to her sister, and referenced small amounts of money that Dot was sending to help take care of Baby Linda. Linda pulled out others that were written to Dot. At some point, apparently in the late 1950s, judging by the dates, Dot had given a collection of her own mail to her sister.

"Looks like saving letters was a family trait," said Angela.

"I didn't know these were here until I started going through the box after you called. Dot must have left them with Mama. Some are beautiful and some are so sad. I want you to keep these, honey, for as long as you want. Your mom will want to look, I'm sure."

Angela agreed. One letter was particularly interesting and she set that aside.

Linda left before dinner. "We both could use some rest," she said. The women embraced for a long time. Angela started to cry again, and Linda joined her. "I am so glad you found me."

"Me, too," Angela said as she finally loosened her hug.

"We'll see each other soon," promised Linda, kissing Angela on the cheek.

The elevator door had not closed behind Linda when two heads popped out of the apartment across the hall. Angela had expected as much, and thanked Stu by letting the men read the letter she had kept out. It was an act she would later regret.

9

As exciting as it was to gain an aunt, and as tragic as it was to lose a friend, Angela had to focus on a more basic economic problem: the future of Pro Traffic. She, Denise, and Justin had become the de facto managers of the company. They met for hours the week following their discovery that Krista had died. There were customers and investors to notify and mountains of paperwork. In addition to the thousand little tasks that required attention, they had to face the major issue of whether and how Pro Traffic would continue without Krista.

Foremost on Angela's mind, of course, was the Chicago bid. Once they decided that Pro Traffic would live beyond its founder, it became clear that winning the contract would be up to her. She realized how inadequate her initial draft presentation had been, and tried to think like Krista in order to fill in the blanks. With that, plus working fifteen-hour days, she was able to create a proposal that Krista would have been proud of.

Denise helped Krista's mother plan the memorial service, which took place at St. Peter's Church in the Loop two weeks to the day after they learned of her death. Krista had been nominally Catholic, but her parents were much more devout and their priest in Ohio knew the pastor at St. Peter's. Afterward, the family returned to Krista's River North condo to continue cleaning and sorting.

The Pro Traffic family was rarely dressed up, and Denise decided they needed to eat something other than yogurt or subs. She organized an early dinner for her co-workers at a trendy place on Madison.

The waiter was pouring wine when Angela felt a kick under the table. It was Denise.

"Look who just walked in," she whispered. Angela looked to the door: it was Bob Stendahl, president of their competitor for the Chicago contract.

He was accompanied by an attractive woman, a few years younger than Stendahl, in a silver cocktail dress. They were with a couple Angela didn't recognize, followed by a woman in a black suit. The maître d' led the party to a corner booth, across the dining room from Pro Traffic's table. Stendahl noticed Angela. He broke away from his group and came over to her.

"Very sorry to hear about Krista." Stendahl's voice was completely neutral. He might have been asking the waiter for sparkling water. Angela wasn't sure whether she would call it cold, but it definitely wasn't warm.

"Thank you." She returned his stare, refusing to be the first to blink. After a long moment, the woman in the black suit approached Stendahl. He took her presence as the opportunity to disengage from Angela. The woman's brown hair was wavy, tucked back behind her ear on one side. She was some decades older than Angela but it wasn't clear how many. Despite her black suit being entirely male, she managed to create an aura that approached feminine. The woman smiled politely at Angela as she turned and followed Stendahl back to his table. Once he was seated, the woman moved about fifteen feet away and stood by a wall, hands in front of her, eyes moving around the room.

"That was strange," Denise was saying. "How does he even know who we are?"

"Good question," Angela replied. "I don't know that he'd ever met Krista. She hadn't mentioned it to me. And check out that bodyguard."

"Where?" Justin spoke loudly enough that even if the woman in the suit hadn't seen him jerk his head she would have heard him. Angela kicked Justin under the table, and Denise reached for the basket of rolls.

"Here," Denise said, handing the rolls to Justin. "The rolls are here."

"But I didn't ask for a roll."

"Justin! Inside voice, please?" Angela glanced briefly toward the woman who was now watching them.

"What? Hey, no need to kick me."

Denise rolled her eyes and sipped the wine. She turned toward Angela.

"The other day you said that you had met a long lost aunt. I've been dying to learn more, but we haven't had a chance. What's the story?"

Angela told her about Stu, and Justin's help to find Aunt Linda.

"What a revelation, to discover what you had known about your family wasn't the whole history," said Denise.

Angela sipped her wine before responding. "It's sad that Grandma Dot never told anyone. Except my grandfather, of course. I mean my biological grandfather. I don't think that Grandpa Dom knew."

"How do you know that?"

"The letters. Aunt Linda had a box of them from her mother. Or, rather the woman who raised her, who turns out to have been Grandma Dot's sister."

"You need a flow chart to keep all this straight." Denise smiled gently. Angela pulled out the pen and paper pad that was always in her purse and started diagramming a family tree. "No, Angela, I was joking. I'm following you. My point was that it's complicated." Angela looked up with a blank look that was quickly replaced with a grin.

"Sorry. I guess I've lost my sense of humor."

"You are under so much stress." Denise put her hand on Angela's arm. "Maybe you can take tomorrow off?"

Tomorrow they needed to work on a problem with the Peoria contract, which Angela had been able to salvage after Krista's death. She couldn't take the day off, and Denise knew that. Angela smiled at her, grateful for the thought anyway.

"Thanks, but I'll be fine. A good night's sleep will help."

As if on cue, the waiter reappeared to fill their wine glasses. The young women picked up their glasses at the same time.

"To a good night's sleep," toasted Denise. "And to family, old and new."

"Not necessarily in that order," Angela replied as they clinked their glasses.

10

In the morning I was early to pick up Bob Stendahl. His wife, Suzi, poured me a cup of coffee while I sat at their kitchen table waiting for him. A really big kitchen table in a really big, gleaming, state of the art kitchen.

Suzi left the room as Bill walked in to debrief me on the night before. This took exactly two seconds. Nothing happened. Just like the last four nights, and the last three days. The most interesting thing that had happened was going with them to a fancy restaurant downtown, and that wasn't particularly interesting. This was, as Bill said, slow duty.

Bill was a big guy, well over six feet tall and built like a Mack truck. He was former Navy and had worked for Charlie since he returned from Afghanistan. During that absence, Bill's wife had moved in with the guy who lived next door. We bonded over bitterness and he taught me a lot about the close protection business. I liked working with Bill. He was cool and professional and didn't mind working nights.

"Do you have any idea why we're here?" I asked for the dozenth time since we'd been in Chicago.

Bill shook his head. He checked his Beretta M9, drained his coffee and stood up.

"See you tonight," I said as he left. Bill wasn't unfriendly. He just wasn't much of a talker.

Bob walked in, past the fancy oven and the extra-wide chrome refrigerator. As he said "good morning," his phone rang. He frowned when he saw the number.

"Hi, Dad," Bob said, and stepped into the dining room. He closed the door behind him. I finished my coffee and placed the cup in the beautifully enameled sink, which put me at least ten feet closer to the dining room door. So I listened. What can I say? I didn't trust these people.

"Who? About that? Dad, that was a long time ago. It can't be." A pause. "We're not having this conversation. Not on the phone. I'll be downtown in forty-five minutes. We can talk then."

I turned on the faucet to rinse my cup as he charged through the door.

"Goldie's?" I asked, as if I hadn't overheard him. This North Shore coffee shop was where he normally began his day.

"No," he growled. Then he recovered. "Straight to the office today." His voice took on a forced brightness. I acted like I hadn't noticed the change.

Our ride downtown was quiet. Green Bay Road through the suburbs, then cutting around Evanston by the lakefront, through Rogers Park past Loyola University, and finally onto the four southbound lanes of Lake Shore Drive. Traffic moved slowly but steadily. The routine of the route made me uncomfortable and I had initially argued with his driver about that. On the third day, just to prove his point, the driver took the expressway rather than Lake Shore Drive. The parking lot in Omaha's Westroads mall at Christmastime was less congested. For a while I'd been afraid that Bob was going to miss a nine o'clock meeting although we'd left his house before seven. Needless to say, I learned the lesson. Lake Shore Drive it would be.

But beyond the route, we hadn't established a pattern yet: sometimes he was chatty, sometimes he talked on his phone, and sometimes he worked on his tablet. Today was a tablet day. I responded to an administrative email from Charlie and started to think about Bob's phone call from Floyd.

My phone buzzed with a text. It was Mark, my boyfriend, of sorts, from New Orleans.

"Can you talk?"

"No. With client." I looked at Bob, who had begun staring out the window. Then he blinked his eyes and returned to his tablet.

"Need to talk. ASAP."

"Can't talk now. What's up?"

"NSFT."

It took me a minute to decipher that one: not safe for
texting. What was he talking about? I wondered whether it had to do
with the research I'd asked him to do on the Stendahls before I came
to Chicago. Mark taught computer science and his hacking skills
rivaled his talents in bed. This time I'd told him not to do anything
that could get him in trouble, but he had checked some legitimate
databases for me. Before I'd gotten on the plane in Miami he
reported that he couldn't find anything suspicious about Bob or
Floyd or the Stendahl Group. From all accounts, they were your
typical run of the mill gazillionaires. Had he found something else?

This was annoying. I wouldn't be able to call until later that
night when Bill relieved me. I glanced at Bob who was focused on his
tablet.

"What???" I texted. I'm not sure why I thought extra
question marks would help.

"Call me."

"Can't until tonight." I sighed, and thought about including
an unhappy emoticon, but that seemed peevish.

"ASAP."

There was no further point to the conversation, so I gazed
out the window. Rush hour traffic on Lake Shore Drive was normal
for seven thirty, which is to say slow but moving. I pushed Mark's
texts out of my mind and returned to Bob's conversation with Floyd.

Had he been forty years younger, Floyd Stendahl would
have scared me. At nearly ninety, his intensity had been reduced by a
slight stoop and the occasional use of a cane. Although sometimes he
came across as the crotchety old guy telling you to stay off his lawn, if
you spent any time with him at all you learned that he was still a force
to be reckoned with.

But even by those standards, he was in high form that
morning, waiting for Bob in the bright white lobby. He stood to the
side of the receptionist's desk where Alissa Marek, a white woman in

her twenties with dark blonde hair and only a bit too much makeup, sat looking more than a little nervous. I didn't blame her.

Floyd said nothing to us because he didn't need to. He glared at Bob, and me, and the room in general, then tilted his head toward his office. Bob immediately moved that direction. It was funny to see the president of a billion-dollar company obey an unspoken order and follow an old man like a plebe, but maybe that's how it is with a dad.

Alissa and I nodded at each other as I followed Bob around the white wall behind her desk. The two men entered Bob's office and shut the door. I stood in front of the door, made of frosted glass that was heavy enough to provide privacy except if people were shouting. Which they were.

"Goddammit, Dad, you're being paranoid. And right now we've got real problems to worry about."

"This is a real problem. The guy's been digging, and for all I know DeLuca's gonna show up again."

"Really? After all these years? Dad, he's dead. He has to be. He's not coming back."

Floyd's voice dropped so I couldn't hear any more. He stormed out of the office, and his cane's thumping as he walked made him more, not less, intimidating. He didn't acknowledge my presence and stomped along the glass wall to his office at the other end of the hall.

The rest of the morning was uneventful. Boring, actually, the way personal security can often be, and the way my time at Stendahl had been. When my principal—that's the person being protected, like Bob—was stationary in a protected space, I had a lot of time to think.

I thought about who DeLuca might be, and where he had been, and for how long, and why Floyd cared. And who was digging up whatever it was that bothered Floyd. I wondered what Mark was in such a hurry to tell me. But most of all I thought about what Bob's real problems were, those that Bob had referred to, the reason why

Mason Security had been retained, at no small expense, to provide twenty-four/seven protection for Bob Stendahl. Those were the problems that he still hadn't told us. Then I thought about why a security firm from Miami had been chosen to protect him against those unspecified problems in the first place.

If you accepted that Bob should want an out-of-town firm, it made sense that he would have picked us. Suzi Stendahl liked Mason Security, or at least, she liked me. That past winter there had been some break-ins in the South Miami Beach neighborhood near the Stendahls' second home. Or maybe it was their fourth home. Anyway, somebody had recommended Mason to her, and Charlie had taken me with him when we met Suzi for the initial walkthrough. A few days after we started protecting their home—which was simply a matter of a few patrols and occasionally parking in their driveway— the burglaries stopped. I was confident this had little to do with us. Charlie took the credit, however, since it was good for business, and who was I to argue? After all, it was enough to land Charlie this very lucrative gig, proving that his mind for business was better than mine.

Since I'd been in Chicago, Suzi had talked with me over coffee a couple of mornings. She used the word "trust" a lot, as in "we weren't sure who in Chicago to trust" and "we trust you." I didn't know whether she knew the details of Bob's real problems. Given the lack of any visible threat during the week that Bill and I had been with him, I had begun to wonder if they were overreacting to something. After hearing Bob's conversation with his father, I wasn't so sure, although I still couldn't answer the question, "overreacting to what?"

I checked my watch. Ten o'clock. Bob's admin walked by to tell me he had a twelve thirty lunch at the nearby restaurant where he ate three days a week. That afternoon he'd be back in the office. A long day of standing around. I was tired of my thoughts being all questions and no answers, so I decided it would be a backwards presidents day. During slow days, I would silently recite all the U.S.

49

presidents to keep my mind occupied but not distracted. During very slow days, I would recite them backwards.

My phone vibrated when my friend Shelly texted me, and I replied "At work." Shelly and I go way back, to when we both lived in Omaha. She had moved to Minneapolis to be near her grandkids and it had been a while since I'd seen her. I did want to catch up, but even on a slow day I wasn't going to text with a friend when I was supposed to be guarding someone.

So I began, with a grimace to start. "Trump, Obama, Bush '43, Clinton, Bush '41..." This was easy until Coolidge, and then I always had to think. For some reason I frequently skipped Harding and went straight to Wilson. Of course, the fact that it was hard was the point. It kept me alert.

I had reached Grover Cleveland for the third time when I heard voices in the lobby. Bob was still at his desk, so I walked down the short hallway and peered around the wall to the reception area.

An old man with a big red nose was arguing with Alissa Marek.

"You cannot see him without an appointment." The strength of her voice surprised me.

"Then I want to make an appointment to see him right now. I left him a voicemail but he won't call me back."

They were going around and around with this. I stepped out from behind the wall.

"Need anything?" I asked Alissa. Her face was flushed, and she looked relieved at my presence.

The old man looked at me, trying to decide if I were an ally or a barricade. "You his secretary?"

"No sir, I'm not. But if you leave your name and phone number with us, we will have his secretary call you to discuss a meeting." That was a lie, of course. But when you need to get rid of someone, a lie can be better than the alternative: physical force.

The lie didn't work. The old man stomped over to the white sofa underneath the white artwork on the white wall and sat down. I was about to ask Alissa to call the building's front desk when he spoke again.

"You can go get him. He'll want to talk to Stu Mackenzie. Tell him that I'm a friend of Larry DeLuca."

11

Normally I would have escorted somebody like Stu Mackenzie to the street and told building security not to let him back in. But hearing the name DeLuca twice in one morning seemed like a reason to interrupt my principal's paperwork, just so Bob knew what was going on. He paled when I said "DeLuca."

"Who is this guy?" Bob shuffled papers on his desk, but his normal color didn't return.

"Stu Mackenzie, he says his name is." I looked at my phone. As usual, Charlie was on top of things, and had just responded to a text I'd sent a minute earlier with Mackenzie's name. Charlie spent a ton of money on several databases, which made up in speed what they lack in technical legality. Between him and Mark, it was amazing what I could discover. "Charlie says he just appears to be some old man. No obvious red flags. He's in his eighties. He wanted to see your dad, but I thought it would be better to tell you first."

"Come in and close the door. Yes, better to tell me first. You say that Mason ran a background check already? That there's nothing on him? Do we know that he's a friend of Larry DeLuca?"

Ten minutes earlier I would have said that Bob Stendahl was the kind of guy who couldn't be rattled. I was wrong. I stood in front of his desk and he closed up some file folders as if he were worried I would see what they contained. His face remained ashen.

"The guy says he is a friend of DeLuca, but that's something we have no way to confirm." I looked at my phone, where Charlie had emailed eight decades of a man's life in thirty seconds.

"He lives on North Winthrop. He's retired, of course. Used to work as a truck driver for a soft drink bottler here in Chicago. Widowed. Served in World War II. Europe. Never arrested, never sued."

Stendahl stared at me as I ticked off Mackenzie's life. "Soft drink bottler? Where else did he work?"

I scrolled further down. "He worked at the Edgewater Beach Hotel. Also in Chicago."

"When?"

"In the forties."

Bob's eyes widened. "And where is he now?"

"I put him in a conference room. The small one, near the kitchen."

"He's not seen my father?"

"Not unless Mr. Stendahl has been by that conference room in the past few minutes. Look, I had to leave him with Tony, so I should get back to him." Tony was a finance guy in the office, whose qualification for watching Mackenzie was that he looked like he lifted weights and had been in the kitchen getting coffee when I plopped Stu into the next room over.

"Yes. I don't want him to see Dad. I'll be down in a minute. And can you please email me whatever you've got on him? I want a copy."

As I walked down the hall I considered whether the Mackenzie/DeLuca situation, as I had started to think of it, was the reason for our assignment. I didn't think so. Bob's call with his father that morning sounded like DeLuca, whoever he was, had popped up unexpectedly. If so, the initial reason—Bob's "real problems"—still were unknown, at least to Bill and me.

Mackenzie urged me to call him Stu as I stood by the door. Tony had gotten him some coffee, and I didn't try to hide my annoyance as I told the young man he could go back to his spreadsheets. Stu Mackenzie was an intruder, not a guest. But to be fair to Tony, Stu looked like a grandfather and it's hard to feel threatened by an octogenarian with a big red nose.

Bob was only a minute behind me, and he had taken that minute to recover his composure. He asked me to stand outside the door and sat down at the table with the old man.

Luckily for me, this conference room had been designed for meetings where proximity to coffee was more important than confidentiality, and the glass door was not soundproof.

"Mr. Mackenzie," Bob began.

"Stu."

"Let's keep this formal, shall we? Why don't you tell me why you're here, and why you insisted on seeing me."

"I don't want to see you. I want to see your dad. *Mister* Stendahl." Mackenzie emphasized "Mister" in a way that confirmed him as a smart aleck and made me smile.

"I am Mr. Stendahl. If you have business with my company, you have business with me. If you don't, then you need to leave."

"I want to see Floyd Stendahl. Either him, or I'm going to talk with the police."

I would say that my ears perked up at the mention of police, but I had already been paying close attention.

"He's not here. Tell me what you want to tell him and I'll give him the message. And don't think you can threaten us."

Quiet for a moment, Mackenzie was apparently considering his options. I heard a chair move on the floor and turned to see the old man standing up.

"Okay, Mr. Stendahl. I'm leaving. If your father isn't man enough to discuss this in person, then to hell with both of you."

The door opened and Stu Mackenzie marched out as I heard Bob start talking into his cellphone. And that was it. I watched Mackenzie give a quick "thank you" to Alissa, and I waited in the lobby until he got on the elevator.

The rest of the day lasted forever. I didn't have enough information to figure out what was going on, and I began to obsess on the meaning of Mark's ominous texts. Not even my backward presidents trick worked to keep my mind occupied. I was glad when Bill relieved me early, meeting us at the office rather than waiting until we returned to the Stendahls' home.

Back at the hotel, I called Mark.

"You won't believe this," he began.

"Try me. I've been thinking all day of the thousands of reasons you needed to talk with me in such a hurry."

He paused, which he liked to do to maximize suspense. Sometimes I found it endearing, but today had been a long day.

"Mark, what?"

"I got a call from the FBI."

"The FBI?"

"Yes. Remember when I was looking up the Stendahls for you?"

"Yeah. You said that nothing unexpected came up."

"That's right. But the fact that I was doing a search about them apparently caught the interest of the Feds."

"Why? And how did they even know you were looking?"

"Tina," Mark said with a tired patience. "They know everything about anything they're interested in. They were monitoring the Stendahls, and when I started hitting a bunch of databases looking for Stendahls, they wanted to know why."

"What did you tell them?"

"The truth. Then they checked your license and Mason Security and I guess they were happy."

"Happy?" My voice started to move to a higher octave. "Did they talk with Charlie?"

"I don't know."

"They must not have talked with him, or he'd have been all over me by now." Then the real point hit me. "Why were they investigating the Stendahls?"

"I didn't say 'investigating.' I said 'monitoring,'" said Mark. "And I asked the FBI guy that same question. Of course, he wouldn't tell me."

"What did he say, exactly?"

"Well, he said he was from cyber terrorism, and that they wanted to know why I was checking into the Stendahls." He paused. "I'm really glad I didn't get into any secure databases."

"Me, too." I shook my head at the thought of how badly that could have gone. "What else did he say? I want to know why they had flagged the Stendahls in the first place."

Mark was silent for a moment. I could almost see his gorgeous dark eyebrows furrow in concentration. "I don't know," he finally said. "I don't know."

12

Bob didn't say anything about Stu Mackenzie after his visit, and of course I didn't ask. Nor did I ask why he thought the Feds would be monitoring him or his company. After the scare with the FBI, I couldn't ask Mark to do any further digging on that topic. I couldn't ask Charlie, either, because the Stendahls were still paying customers. Not only did my online sources dry up, but the human ones did, too. Nobody said or did anything that provided a clue as to why Bill and I were protecting the Stendahls.

One bright spot—in addition to the fact that the job still beat telemarketing hands down—was meeting Bob's cousin, Tom Donnelly. He ran the construction side of the business and was such an easy-going guy that at first I thought Bill was joking when he told me he and Bob Stendahl were related.

Tom was a little older than me, which is to say in his mid-fifties. His hair was the kind you want to run your fingers through, with the beginning of gray starting to appear among soft brown curls. And no, these were not the thoughts I was supposed to have about clients. Luckily I didn't see him much the first couple of weeks I was there; his offices were in an industrial section of Chicago, a few miles northwest of the Loop. Bob grumbled about that, mentioning a couple of times that they were too far away from the rest of the Stendahl Group. He did this once in Floyd's presence, and Floyd shot him a "we've discussed this and I don't care about your opinion" look.

But one morning in late June as we left his house, Bob told the driver to drop me at Stendahl Construction.

"I need you to stay with Tom this morning. Take a look around the construction yard and tell him what to do to tighten up security. I'll come get you after lunch."

"Should I call Bill to have him pick you up? You're the principal, after all." Bill wouldn't have gone to sleep yet, and while he wouldn't have been thrilled about extending his tour another half day, he was a professional and would agree we shouldn't leave our client unguarded.

"No, no need for that. I'll be fine."

"Sir, are you certain?" I'd only had a principal do this one other time in my year at Mason, and it had seemed pretty clear he'd been meeting a mistress. Bob had shown no such inclinations, but principals don't drop their highly paid security details for no reason. I would report this to Charlie and Bill, of course, although Charlie was unlikely to fight a client. I resolved to focus on securing the assets of Stendahl Construction, not including Tom's hair.

Which turned out to be relatively easy for a while. The offices were in the middle of a storage yard surrounded by an eight-foot chain link fence. A young superintendent and I spent a couple of hours walking through the property while I showed him how to better protect the equipment they stored there.

I sat down in the mid-Seventies era break room to spec out improvements to their security plans and Tom offered me some iced tea. It was unnerving to be attracted to a client, so I tried to find something repulsive about him that I could focus on. Unsuccessful, I decided to see if he might have some insight into the FBI question, or why his cousin had hired us, or both.

"Things have seemed pretty quiet since we got here," I commented as Tom stirred some sweetener into my tea. He set the stadium cup on the white Formica table where I sat, then plopped onto a brown plastic chair across from me.

"They usually are. Not much excitement at a construction office."

"No, I mean Stendahl Group in general," I said.

"Well, there's generally not a lot of excitement downtown, either."

"Hmm." I sipped my tea.

Tom examined his cup, a memento of a Blackhawks hockey playoff game. I set mine down as if I were anticipating an answer.

Which I was. It's amazing how often someone will say something they're reluctant to say simply because they're more uncomfortable with silence.

"Then you're probably wondering why Bob hired you?"

I nodded. The key here was to keep the pressure on by staying quiet. Tom found the hockey pictures on his cup especially fascinating, but I could outwait him. I had until after lunch, at least.

"Bob had a transaction with a customer that has made us all a bit…unsettled."

I looked at him over my tea as I took another sip.

He closed his eyes when he took a drink, then opened them to stare at the Blackhawks again. "They're Russian."

I thought I knew what he meant, but as long as he was willing to talk, it wouldn't hurt to be sure. This time I didn't nod. That would have let him think he was finished, and he wasn't.

"Bob said that it started out with legitimate people, but then these other guys came in."

I waited. Tom took a long drink. I waited. One more drink and he emptied the cup. He wasn't going to say it.

"Organized crime?" I asked.

He nodded.

"So why am I here right now?"

"I just told you." He stood up and walked to the sink.

"No, I mean why am I in your office rather than protecting Bob?"

Tom set his cup in the sink and grabbed the edge of the chipped counter with both hands. He leaned forward a little, and I went over to him.

"Are you okay?"

"Yes. I'm fine."

"You don't look fine. What's wrong? Tom, we can't protect him if nobody tells us what's going on."

"It's worse than organized crime. That's only part of it."

"What's the rest?"

"The sale itself. You've heard of ITAR? International Traffic in Arms Regulation? It's a federal law that limits the sale of technology to foreign countries like Russia."

I hadn't heard of it, and given that the superintendent had just walked into the room I wasn't going to for a while.

13

When Angela got an email from the assistant to the City of Chicago's assistant purchasing director the morning of their presentation, she knew it wasn't going to be good news.

"They've rescheduled us to next month," she wailed to Denise. Justin, who had gone to the considerable trouble of procuring a suit and clean shirt for the occasion, looked up from his monitor with an expression between frustration and fear.

"Let me see," said Denise. She and Justin both ran to Angela's laptop.

"They're putting us off." Angela picked up the phone for what she knew would be a fruitless effort. Denise and Justin stood behind her while she did a reasonable impersonation of someone who wasn't desperate talking with the assistant to the assistant purchasing director. She shook her head as she hung up the phone.

"Christ." Justin took off his jacket and loosened his tie. Angela and Denise looked at each other: this was the strongest statement Justin had ever made in their presence.

"So now what?" Denise asked as she flopped into a chair. A couple of the developers had overheard and messaged their earbudded coworkers. Everybody in the office was looking at them.

"It's not great," Angela admitted. "But I'm not giving up. They're going to have to work harder than this to stop us. We'll just figure out another way. For Krista, and for us." She stood up, wishing she felt half as confident as her words. Several investors had expressed concern about the future of the company post-Krista. Their cash flow had been tight, and Angela spent time every week juggling the company's bills. She hadn't had to lay anyone off yet, but without new business, they were in trouble.

Denise followed her into the bathroom and they hugged each other while they cried.

"What can we do?" Denise sniffed into Angela's shoulder.

"I don't know. We'll think of something. But we need to keep everything else together. The team needs us."

"It's not over yet," Denise said.

Angela squeezed her in thanks, then backed away enough to hold Denise by her shoulders. "No, not by a long shot. It's not over until we say it is!" Angela's voice cracked as she said it.

Denise handed a tissue to Angela and used one herself. Angela recovered first.

"I think I'll just go to City Hall this afternoon," she said. "And I'll talk with that alderman's aide. They need to know we won't quit easily."

"Thattagirl!" Denise punched her shoulder as they walked out of the bathroom. Angela returned the blow with a laugh and the women continued their fake fight down the short hall to Pro Traffic's office.

They stopped as they saw a heavyset man in their doorway. Justin was walking toward him and looked confused. The company rarely had visitors.

"May I help you?" Justin asked, as Denise and Angela approached the man from behind.

"Yes. Detective James Logan, CPD." He flipped an ID to Justin and turned as he sensed the women behind him. He was the African-American detective they had met a few weeks earlier.

Angela held out her hand. "Angela Frank. We met at the station. And you remember Denise Glover. This is Justin Navarro, our director of system development."

The rest of the developers were staring.

"Justin, can you please tell the guys that everything is fine? We'll speak with Detective Logan in the conference room." Angela ushered him into a small room created by using frosted glass to divide what had formerly been a corner of the office. There was theoretically room for six people—six skinny people. Given Detective Logan's size, Angela was glad they wouldn't be at capacity.

The detective declined Denise's invitation for coffee as he sat by the door, where he wouldn't need to squeeze himself along a wall.

"We haven't heard anything," Denise said with more than a bit of accusation in her voice. She had called the CPD every couple of days after their initial meeting, until the officer answering the phone told her in no uncertain terms to stop.

"No, there's not been much to report." If Detective Logan felt accused, his voice didn't let on. "Until yesterday."

Angela, Denise, and Justin all leaned forward.

"Yesterday we were able to arrest the people running the car theft ring. That's the good news. They'd been running this for a number of months, and because of Ms. Jordan, we were able to close the case."

Denise broke first.

"Okay, that's great. But what happened to Krista? Was her..." Denise paused before she could say the word. "Was her death linked to the car thefts?"

"No. That's the bad news. We still don't know why your friend was killed. But we continue to be certain that she was killed deliberately, that it wasn't an accident. The damage to the rear of the vehicle indicated her car was pushed off the road by another vehicle." He looked at his notes and looked up at the women. "You stated that it was unlike Ms. Jordan not to carry her driver's license?"

Angela nodded.

"The fact that her identification was missing proves either that Ms. Jordan left it elsewhere, which we agree is unlikely, or that someone took it."

"Presumably whoever killed her? To slow down the identification?" Angela asked.

Detective Logan nodded. He flipped open his notepad.

"Since we have determined that involvement in the car theft ring—" he lifted his hand to Denise's immediate objection and corrected himself, "—as a blameless party is not the motive in Ms.

Jordan's death, we're back to square one. That's why I'm here. Can you think of anyone—business, personal, whoever—who was angry with Ms. Jordan, or who would benefit from her death? Ms. Jordan had family in Ohio, I believe. Her brother was named the beneficiary in her will, but it does not appear that she had significant assets."

"Except for her ownership interest in Pro Traffic," Angela said. She didn't mean it to sound as defensive as it did.

"Yes, of course. Are there other owners?"

"Denise, can you please get a cap table for Detective Logan?" Angela asked. "That's a list of owners," she explained to the detective as Denise stepped out. "There are a number of investors, plus the three of us each have a small equity stake."

"And now that Ms. Jordan is dead, what happens to the company? The remaining owners split up Ms. Jordan's share?"

"Yes. It's all spelled out in the investment documents. But it's not that simple, because with Krista gone, the value of the company has declined. We're working on some big prospects, but she was our best salesperson. She was going to Peoria to close a deal when she was killed. I was barely able to get that sale done without her. We have some good long-term contracts, but growing the business became a lot harder when she died. So although everyone now technically owns a bigger piece of the pie, the pie itself may have shrunk. Or, at least, it's not growing the way everyone counted on."

Detective Logan made some notes, and nodded to Denise as she returned with the list of owners.

"Anybody else? A boyfriend, an ex-boyfriend, a girlfriend?"

Denise sat back down. "She was seeing a guy named Dan Foster. Sort of on again, off again, but it never seemed so serious that he would get upset enough to do something like this." Denise and Angela had discussed this before and agreed that Foster was unlikely to be the killer.

"You ever meet this guy?"

"He stopped in sometimes. He works somewhere in the Loop and would bring her lunch or dinner." Angela looked at Denise, thinking she might know where Foster worked.

"Kiel Schwedland." It was the first time Justin had spoken since they entered the conference room.

"Excuse me?" Detective Logan looked at him.

"Kiel Schwedland. It's a small investment house."

Angela and Denise stared at Justin.

"What?" he asked defensively. "I pay attention to this stuff. Krista had wanted them to invest in us but we were still too early. At least, that's what he told her one night when he was over here."

"Really? Why didn't she tell us?" Angela had thought Krista had confided in her about all their investment prospects.

Justin shrugged. "I think she thought I wasn't listening. But just because I've got the earbuds in doesn't mean I can't hear you."

Angela shook her head, smiling despite herself.

Detective Logan passed his cards out like he was dealing poker, asked them one more time if they could think of anyone who might have wanted to kill Krista, maneuvered himself out of the chair, and left.

14

Angela's Saturday morning peace and quiet—and coffee—
was interrupted by an insistent knock at her door. She wasn't
surprised that it was Les, although his expression was unexpected.
Red eyes, no smile: he looked like a man who'd just lost his best
friend.

"Stu's dead, Angie."

She ushered him in, gave him a hug, and poured him coffee.
Les made his way into her living room and sat down.

"I'm very sorry. He looked fine last time I saw him." Angela
handed Les a steaming mug.

"He was fine. He didn't die from being sick. It was a hit-
and-run. Somebody hit Stu and left him…"

Angela reached for a tissue and traded it to Lester for his
coffee. He blew his nose as a way to cover his wet eyes. She set the
coffee on the coffee table in front of him, then grabbed a tissue for
herself.

"Les, I am so sorry. How horrible. When did it happen?"

"Yesterday. Over on Broadway. He was crossing the street."
Angela handed him more tissues and he broke down in earnest.

Angela wasn't sure what to say and finally arrived at, "He
was such a great guy. I'm glad you introduced us." She dabbed at her
eyes, handed Lester more tissues and waited. They sat for a while,
and then Les recovered enough to begin recounting stories of Stu.
He even drank some of the coffee.

"He really liked you," Lester eventually said.

"I liked him, too," said Angela. "And I'm so grateful that he
told me about my grandmother, and Aunt Linda."

Les nodded. "That letter you showed us…that was really
something."

"It was. To think that Grandma Dot and Larry DeLuca,
Grandpa Larry, had witnessed a murder. And that was why Grandpa

Larry had to leave." Angela looked out the window, then back at Lester. "Well, at least one of the reasons."

"Stu had asked me what you were going to do about that letter," Lester said.

"Nothing. You know, Aunt Linda worked for the CPD for a long time. She was a secretary. She said that there was no way they'd pay attention to an accusation from so long ago, in a letter from a man who's probably dead, against somebody like Floyd Stendahl."

"Stu thought it was important evidence. He said he wanted to check something out and then he would talk with you about going to the police."

"What was it?"

"I don't know. And now we'll never know, will we?" Lester's voice cracked.

Angela leaned toward him, gently removing the cooled cup from his curled fingers. She rested her hand on his knee, and felt his body shake as he fought back tears.

They sat that way for a while. After a few minutes, Lester stopped shaking and stood up.

"Thank you for the coffee. You're very nice to your old neighbor, but I know you're busy. I'll let you get on with your day."

"Lester, no, you don't need to go. If you want to be around someone, please feel free to stay. I've got more coffee."

"No." He shook his head miserably. "I think I need to be alone right now. I'm really going to miss that crazy guy."

Angela stood up and embraced him. She walked the old man to her door with her arm around his shoulders. He reached for the door knob and she gave him a soft squeeze.

"You're a good girl, Angie. Thank you."

"And you're a good man, Lester. I'm really sorry that you lost a friend."

Lester said nothing as he padded across the hall to his apartment.

Angela refilled her coffee and picked up the box of tissues. Sad and reflective from the news about Stu, she decided to reread the letters that Larry DeLuca had sent her grandmother. Aunt Linda's cardboard box was on the floor in her bedroom, and she sat on the rug by her bed to look through them again, her eyes tearing up.

Larry DeLuca wrote in a cramped hand, without paragraphs.

"Sweet Dot, I miss you terribly. The sun in Mexico is hot, but without your beautiful smile I'm afraid I'll never be warm again. Are you sure you can't join me? If only we hadn't been at the bar that night, everything would be different. Floyd Stendahl killed one man, but he took my life the same as if he'd knifed me, too, by making me leave you. I wish we could fight them, but people like us can't fight people like them. The best we can hope is that he holds up his end of the deal. I love you and hold you in my dreams."

That was the letter she had showed Stu, knowing that the mystery would appeal to him. She wondered what he was poking into, and whether he'd been able to find out anything before he died. She sighed. Lester was right: they'd never know.

There were several letters, all from 1949, the year of Dot's pregnancy, her marriage to Dom, and Joyce's birth.

"My dearest Dot, I heard you were getting married to Dom. If I can't take care of you then I'm glad he will. You are such a special lady that you need two men to love you, and I will always be one of them."

Tears welled up in Angela's eyes. She looked at the last sheet, knowing that it would open the floodgates.

"Dot, I got your letter. I'm sorry that you don't want me to write anymore, but I understand. You are a married woman with a baby. It's just that I love you so much. My soul aches for what we had together. I will respect your wishes, but know that you and our baby will always be in my heart. Yours forever, Larry."

15
Detective Logan

Detective James Logan's twenty-five years on the Chicago Police Department, fifteen of them as a detective, had worn away any delusion he might have once had about the basic goodness of humanity. He had not, however, entirely lost his faith in luck. Every so often there would be some unexpected little break, and a case that had stumped him would start to fall into place. It didn't happen regularly, of course, but it happened enough that he allowed himself to hope for it.

And so it was the last Monday morning in June, as he cleared a small space on his desk for a paper cup of rotgut coffee and considered which file to attack first. The phone rang, and it only took him a few seconds to dig it out from under the stack of papers.

"Logan here." He took a sip of coffee and grimaced.

"Detective Logan, this is Detective Gomez, Sixth District." Vaguely Latino accent, not anyone Logan knew.

"And what can I do for my friends in Gresham this morning?" Logan sincerely hoped that the answer was "nothing." He had enough of his own work to keep him busy.

"Ah, it's what I can do for you today." Logan could nearly hear the smile on the other end of the line. "We picked up a male black, twenty, in a drug sweep. He's a frequent flier, and is looking at more years than he cares to serve."

"You'll have that," Logan said drily, but he set his coffee cup down and picked up a notebook, which conveniently had been sitting on top of a working pen.

"Yes, it happens. But here's the good news for you: this guy says that he knows about a couple of hit-and-runs. One's showing in the system as a presumed homicide, and it's yours." Gomez paused, perhaps looking at his notes. "Krista Jordan. Ring a bell?"

Logan smiled. Sometimes luck was all a man had to hold onto, and sometimes that was enough.

"Yeah, that's mine."

"One question: looks like the death occurred in Livingston County downstate. Why are you working it?"

"Victim was involved with a car theft ring up here, so I just started looking at it."

"Involved? How?"

Things must be slow on the South Side this morning, Logan thought. "She was driving a stolen car. Turns out she'd rented it. That was the ring: they'd steal cars, then rent them to people who thought they were ride-sharing. I don't think that it ended up having anything to do with her death. It just made it a lot harder to identify her body, and the State Police seemed to lose interest."

"The reason I wondered is because my guy's stolen some cars in addition to drug dealing."

"A real Renaissance man." The coffee was still hot, and didn't taste as bad to Logan as it had three minutes earlier.

Gomez snorted. "Yeah. So, d'ya want this guy? I'll hold him here if you're interested. He seems pretty anxious to talk."

"I'll bet he is." Logan took another sip, hung up the phone, and headed to South Halsted.

Detective Gomez escorted Detective Logan to a small interview room, opened the door for him, and wandered away. *My problem now,* Logan thought. *Or, rather, my good luck.* The skinny African-American kid sitting shackled to the metal table looked up as he entered.

"Deshawn Jackson?"

The kid nodded. "You the one investigating that woman downstate? And that old man in Uptown?"

Logan didn't answer and sat at the table across from the kid, placing a manila folder between them. He opened his notebook to a blank page and readied his pen.

"Tell me what you know. Start with the woman." He had no idea what old man in Uptown the kid was talking about, and he didn't care much. First things first.

"Are you gonna make this go away? The other detective said you could."

"Maybe. Depends on whether you tell me something I don't already know."

The kid sat. Logan waited. He counted to himself, the one-one hundred, two-one hundred counting that children did. It was a little game he played. In Logan's experience, if someone didn't talk by forty-one hundred, it meant he—or she—wasn't going to say anything. Since Deshawn had offered information, Logan hoped that the kid wouldn't change his mind. He needn't have worried. Not today. At fifteen-one hundred, Deshawn opened his mouth.

"My man was telling me that he and another guy had gotten paid, big money, to follow this woman downstate and run her off the road."

Deshawn looked at Logan, hoping for a response. Logan withheld and began counting to himself again. *Eight one-hundred. Nine-one hundred.*

"It was a silver Camry."

Logan now had to remind himself to keep counting. He was only a so-so poker player.

"On I-55. Down by Bloomington."

Logan decided the kid had earned a response. "Your man's name?"

"Nooky."

"Real name."

"Shit, man, I don't know. Everybody calls him Nooky."

Logan could check with Gomez on the name, so he went another direction. "How'd Nooky do it?"

The kid stared blankly. "Shit, I don't know. He didn't tell me that."

"What *did* he tell you?"

"That she was pretty. Real pretty. White woman."

"How'd he know she was pretty if he was driving behind her?"

"He said they had to, um, make sure she was dead. And they had to bring her ID to the guy who hired him."

"Make sure she was dead? Do you mean Nooky killed her?"

Deshawn paused, staring at the metal table. He looked up at Logan and nodded.

Bingo. Logan allowed the kid the glimpse of a smile. "So who'd he say the guy was who hired him?"

The kid had been bolstered by Logan's response, and uttered a stream of bullshit that made Logan close up his notebook and begin the slow process of lifting himself out of the chair.

"Look, kid, I don't need to hear about some guy who knows some rich white dude downtown. That's not helpful. That's not valuable." He emphasized the last word, but Jackson didn't speak. "Kid, if you don't give me somebody's name besides Nooky there's nothing I can do to help you with your problems."

Jackson's face showed a struggle between two competing fears: likely prison, or the risk of naming names. Logan had seen this expression before, and it often ended with the witness deciding prison was the safer choice. But this time the witness, Jackson, had stepped forward, at least in a manner of speaking. Maybe this time Logan could get an answer.

"Mr. Jackson, you were the one who told us you could help solve this case. You're looking at real prison time if you don't. Why don't you just finish what you started?"

Jackson looked like he was going to be sick, closed his eyes for a minute, and blurted out "Terrance."

Now the kid had Logan's attention.

"Terrance who?" But Logan knew who. There was only one Terrance anybody on the South Side would be that scared of.

"Terrance Jones."

"Really? And what did Mr. Terrance Jones have to do with this?" Logan settled back in his chair.

The kid managed to look both satisfied and terrified at the same time. "He was the guy. Nooky was driving, but Terrance Jones set it up."

"Well, Deshawn, that is interesting information. Maybe even valuable. I'll make sure to tell Detective Gomez that you've been very cooperative." He started to push himself out of the small chair again.

"Wait, you don't care about the other one?"

"What other one?" Logan had completely forgotten.

"That old man in Uptown. On Broadway. Last week. You may think it was just an accident, but Nooky told me: he and Jones did it. For the same people."

16

I spent the weekend camped out in Bob and Suzi Stendahl's second floor guest room. Very posh. Bill got what Suzi called "the grandkids' room" in the basement, which wasn't too bad, either. Lucky grandkids.

Once I had learned what the Stendahl Group was up to—more specifically, once I realized who they'd pissed off—Bill, Charlie and I insisted on double-teaming. Charlie had convinced Bob that we had to bring in an extra crew. But Charlie was in the middle of staffing some sort of diplomatic conference and didn't have any free guys until the middle of the week. In the meantime, we were putting Bob and Suzi on the voluntary equivalent of house arrest.

They were remarkably good sports, at least at first. Suzi, as it turned out, was a terrific cook. It was nice to have gourmet meals. She even made us brunch on Sunday. Bob worked from his home office much of the weekend. Bill and I overlapped shifts with a few hours here and there to sleep. We weren't sure exactly what we were up against, but when Tom Donnelly had told me about the Russians, our caution flags went up. Suzi seemed to view our presence as reassuring, and since we didn't get in Bob's way much, he tolerated it.

Monday was when Bob became difficult.

"I've got a meeting downtown this afternoon and I need to be there in person," he announced.

"Mr. Stendahl, I'm sorry. It's not a good idea," I said. Bill always let me be the one to talk with the clients.

"But last week was fine."

"Yes. We've been lucky that nothing has happened so far. But luck has a way of running out. You thought the Russians were enough of a threat that you've hired us to protect you, right? Charlie's been working his sources over the weekend to figure out exactly what's going on, since I don't think you've told us the whole story.

We need to know that the situation, whatever it is, has been resolved before we'll feel comfortable returning to business as usual."

"What sources? Who is he telling what? This is a confidential business matter."

Bill looked at me with half a smile. We both had little tolerance for crap. Bill rarely said anything but he liked watching me call it out.

"Mr. Stendahl, you sold illegal technology to Russia, and somehow you've gotten crosswise with the Russian mob. This is not a small thing. Charlie has a couple of contacts and is trying to figure out what we can do to remove the threat. Much as Charlie would love for you to pay him for our services until the end of time, we cannot protect you forever. We need to figure out how to end this."

Bill's phone rang. "Charlie," he answered. "Can I put you on speaker?"

"I've got bad news," Charlie began as we surrounded the phone. "The Russian government believes that you were trying to cheat them, Mr. Stendahl."

Bob started to protest but for a change Bill raised his hand to let Charlie continue.

"Whether they're correct is not the point. The point is that they've engaged Vladimir Orlov to, um, represent them."

"Who is that?" Bob scowled.

"He's one of the major players in the Russian mafia, based in New York. We've come across him in Miami a few times. He has several crews who work for him. They're all as brutal as he is."

For once, Bob had nothing to say.

"I need to advise you to report this to the FBI, Mr. Stendahl," Charlie said.

Bob was quiet for another minute, then shook his head. "No, I can't. Let's open the kimono. Look, we sold the Russians technology we weren't supposed to. And we sold them a lot of it. I could do twenty years in federal prison. Jesus, *Dad* could go to prison. To say nothing of the fines. No Feds."

"I had a feeling you'd say that," said Charlie. "I always advise my clients to follow the law, but I also always have a Plan B."

Bob's face relaxed a little, but Bill's tightened up. We were usually "Plan B."

"Based on what I've been told, the Russians want seven million dollars, which is apparently the amount they think you owe them. And Orlov's job is to collect it from you. He views his collection fee as another seven million, so he wants fourteen million dollars." Charlie waited for Bob's response, which was not forthcoming.

"Is there a way to get Orlov to reduce his fee?" I finally asked. I had a feeling that Bob wanted to know but wasn't sure how to ask in a way that didn't sound cheap and petty with his life—and probably Suzi's and his dad's—at risk.

"Maybe. That's what I've been working on. Mr. Stendahl, is there a number you'd be comfortable with?"

Stendahl slowly shook his head. "You don't understand. The Russians may be telling your sources"—Bob had recovered and now spoke disdainfully—"that they're owed seven million dollars, but the entire transaction was ten times that. And that's what they really want. They aren't going to be happy until they get all of it, and I don't have seventy million dollars. If your Plan B is that I pay them, you're as big an idiot as I've ever met. I know I've got a huge problem; I've hired you to fix it. So fix it."

Charlie was quiet for a moment, as he always was before dropping a bomb. Bill and I both tensed up.

"Orlov is in Chicago," he finally said. "Flew in last night. It sounds like he's got a couple of his guys with him. You need to remain at your house, where we can protect you. We're working on fixing this, Mr. Stendahl, but we need your cooperation."

Bob was silent.

"Got it?" asked Charlie, more harshly than I'd heard him talk to a client before. If Charlie was that alarmed, this was serious.

"Yeah, got it." Bob punched the red button on Bill's phone, ending the call.

Bill and I looked sharply at Bob. The anger had drained from his face. He looked as pale as he had when Stu Mackenzie barged into the office.

"Suzi. Where is she?" he asked.

I hadn't seen her since we'd begun our conversation. "Look in your bedroom and the bathrooms," I told Bob. Bill took the first floor and I checked outside.

The front of the house was quiet, what you'd expect in a wealthy suburb after the commuters had left and before the maids showed up. A dark sedan drove by. Its speed—or, rather, lack of speed—made me uncomfortable. Any car that belonged in the neighborhood would have been trying to make up somebody's last five minutes of dawdling on the way to the office. This car was driving slowly, steadily, in a way that allowed its occupants to observe the area through tinted windows.

No Suzi.

I went around the side of the house, past the hedges that Suzi used as the front boundary for her flower beds. Thirty feet away, there she was, kneeling on a bright yellow pad, pulling weeds. I crossed the lawn toward her. She heard me call her name and turned, brushing the dirt off pink gloves.

"Tina!" She smiled as I approached. "What a lovely morning."

"Mrs. Stendahl, we need to get you back inside. There have been a couple of developments I need to tell you about."

Her smile faded, which I expected. What I didn't expect was her frown becoming a scream. I began to turn around. Somebody grabbed my waist from behind. I tried to spin toward the attacker, but before I got far a fist appeared in front of my face. The hand opened and the last thing I saw was a white cloth coming toward my nose and my mouth. I heard Suzi Stendahl cry out, then nothing.

17

It took most of the day, but by late afternoon Detective Logan was finally ready to interview Terrance Jones. Had it been only a matter of walking into Jones's office, a beaten-down bar on West 63rd, he'd have stopped by at lunch. But Logan wasn't going to get his ass chewed over not following protocol, and Terrance Jones was the subject of a long-standing federal task force. So he made his calls and sent his emails. Besides, he had other logistics to get organized. Finally he received permission to question Jones.

Logan had never met Jones, but everyone in the CPD, as well as avid readers of the *Tribune* and *Chicago Sun-Times*, knew him by reputation. He was widely presumed to be responsible for much of the drug dealing that occurred between the Stevenson Expressway and 95th Street, and the rest of the crime that went along with it. No one on the task force had delusions that he limited his bad behavior to one part of town, no matter how large, but no one knew of anything specific outside the South Side, and even there they'd had trouble making charges stick. So when Logan had told the federal agent heading the task force the purpose of his inquiry, the guy had been curious.

"Go ahead," the agent had said. "You're not going to be in the way of anything we're currently looking into. And it won't hurt for Jones to have a little random visit from CPD—it might help keep him on his toes. Let me know what you find."

There was more to Logan's plan than a random visit, of course. But the agent hadn't asked, and Logan decided not to mention the rest. His butt was covered with the emails, and that was good enough.

Now, as Logan let his eyes adjust to the dark of the bar, he saw who he was looking for, a group of people around a table in the back. There were three men sitting and another three standing, all of them focused on a thirty-something African-American man with his back to the wall. The man was completely without distinguishing features: average short dark hair, average-looking face, and when he stood up as Logan approached, average height. But the way he held court with these men, Logan would have known him even if the detective had not seen photographs in the voluminous file.

"Terrance Jones?" This was an unnecessary question, but Logan liked to play things straight.

Jones motioned and the men with chairs sat down. The men without moved around the table to stand closer to Jones, facing Logan. Everybody's faces tightened, including, Logan thought, his own.

"This is my place," Jones said by way of an answer.

"Are you Terrance Jones?"

"Who are you?"

"Detective James Logan, CPD. I wanted to ask Mr. Jones some questions."

Jones laughed. "The answer for today is twelve."

"Twelve?"

"Twelve, or purple. Or George Washington. Those are my three answers to any questions you want to ask. Just fill them in wherever you'd like."

A couple of the men snickered.

Logan couldn't resist a smile. He made a notation in his notebook.

"Well, Mr. Jones, that certainly is helpful. But I do have something else I wanted to ask you about."

"You with the task force?"

"No sir, I'm not." Logan had worked street crime for years before making detective. He had learned that giving a person more respect than the person deserved was a generally sound strategy for gaining cooperation. "I'm investigating a couple of hit-and-runs. One was downstate and one was in Uptown. I've been told that you may know something about them."

Jones pretended to contemplate the question. "Hit-and-runs? No, doesn't sound familiar. Any of you guys know anything about any hit-and-runs?"

His posse didn't bother pretending before shaking their heads in the negative. No one took his eyes off Logan.

Logan scribbled something in his notebook.

"Well, I guess my information was incorrect. Thanks for clearing that up, and have a nice evening."

He walked calmly out of the bar, pulling at his shirt collar as the late afternoon sun hit him. Summer had arrived in a blast of heat, and it wasn't the kind of weather that favored a big man. Logan felt better when he reached his old sedan and got the air conditioning cranked up. Just one more stop. If things worked out right, it would be worth the price of eating yet another reheated dinner at ten o'clock.

18

I was lying on my side, and the only thing I could see for a minute was a stained white cloth on the clammy, dirty cement floor next to my face. For a moment, maybe longer, I was so woozy that all I could do was lie there. Finally, I gained consciousness enough to notice a rat standing about five feet away, looking at me. Knowing that he considered me fair game provided the motivation I needed to shake myself fully awake.

My arms were bound behind my back, and my feet were tied as well. My head ached, like a hangover. The only light in the dark room came from a single source. I blinked a few times: it was a window, mostly boarded, near the ceiling, that allowed in a few weak glints. I was in a basement.

The rat continued looking at me and began to approach. The adrenalin from that threat allowed me to kick at him with my bound legs, like some sort of deranged mermaid. He moved back cautiously, but he never took his eyes from me. He hadn't conceded yet.

I rolled onto my back and sat up. A wave of nausea hit me before I could do anything more than turn my head, and I was sick. The odor from it nearly made me vomit again, but despite that I felt better.

My eyes were starting to adjust to the light, and I saw the rat scamper off. Now that I had a full field of vision, I saw Suzi Stendahl, also tied up, lying face up on the floor a few feet away.

"Mrs. Stendahl," I whispered. "Can you hear me?"

Of course she couldn't. I saw the mask on her nose and mouth, presumably soaked with the same thing that had kept me knocked out. The light was too dim to see if her chest was moving. I drew my legs underneath me and rose onto my knees. Although my ankles were bound, I could maneuver by moving one knee toward

Suzi, then bringing the other knee in. It took a minute, but I was able to scoot over and pull the mask down so it hung at her neck.

"Mrs. Stendahl?" Nothing, but I could see she was breathing. I struggled with my hands, unable to break the plastic zip ties around my wrists. I hoped it wouldn't take long for her to wake up, and began to wonder how my mask had fallen free. I did my knee walk back to where the mask lay. It was a cheap one, made of paper with a thin elastic band. The band was broken. Broken, or chewed through? I shuddered at the thought of the rat nibbling around my head, and reflexively looked toward the brick wall where he'd last been. Despite the horror of it, if it hadn't been for the rat, I probably still would have been unconscious.

There was a rumbling outside. About thirty seconds, and it passed. Occasionally I heard a shout in the distance. We were near people, maybe in a neighborhood.

I studied the window. One of the boards had slipped, which accounted for the light. It was not bright yellow daylight, so I concluded it was early evening. We'd been out for a while.

There were wooden stairs about ten feet away from where Suzi lay. A couple of the planks were missing. None of them looked particularly solid, although they must have been stable enough to have gotten us down there. The door at the top was closed. I couldn't hear any sounds beyond it, no talking or moving around, and I didn't see any light shining under the door. Perhaps we were alone in the building?

After a few minutes Suzi moaned a little. "Tina? Where are we?"

"I'm working on that. Are you okay?" I knee-walked toward her.

"I think so. Just bruised. I have a headache, and I feel really sick to my stomach."

"Can you sit up?"

"No, I don't think so," she responded after a long pause. "Guess I shouldn't have quit Pilates class." It was reassuring to know that she could crack a joke, even if it were gallows humor.

I responded with a quiet laugh. "Okay. We're in a basement, but I don't know where. What was the last thing you remember seeing?"

She took a minute to answer, then spoke slowly.

"You were coming toward me, and said something. That we had to go inside, I think. Yes, that's what you said. And then I saw two men come from behind the front shrubs, and one of them grabbed you and put something over your mouth. I got up to run to the backyard but stumbled and somebody grabbed me. Then one of them put something over my mouth. I don't remember anything after that."

We both had the same thought, and she said it first.

"Bob! And Bill! Where are they?"

"I don't know. I don't see them in here. I need to find if there's a way out." I was proud of Suzi for staying calm, when someone else in her situation might have become hysterical. "Suzi, how's your manicure?"

"My what?"

"Your fingernails. How long are they?"

"I don't know, normal long, I guess."

"Are your gardening gloves still on?"

"Yes."

"Can you pull your thumb out? Loosen the glove so we can get it off?"

Her shoulders wiggled while she moved her hands behind her back.

"I've got one thumb out," she reported in a whisper.

"Good. Now loosen that glove as much as you can and roll so your back is toward me, so that I can get to your hands."

Still no noise from above us, just the occasional rumble outside. I bent down to get my mouth to her gloved hands, and pulled the glove off with my teeth. Good news: the gloves had kept the zip ties from being too tight around her wrists so she could move her hands a little.

"Okay, this is the hard part, but you're the one with the long nails," I said. "You know how zip ties work, right? There's a plastic bar that locks the teeth and keeps them from going backward? Put your fingernail in there and use it as a shim to lift that bar off the track. Then it should slide out. Roll back toward me so you can get my hands free."

This was easier said than done, of course, and it took Suzi a few tries, but in less than five minutes she had both my hands and feet free. My fingernails were in no condition to be used as shims, not extending beyond my fingertips. But once freed, I used a sliver from a collapsed stair and had her out in a jiffy. She didn't like the next part, where I told her to lay back down. I rebound her, although loosely enough that she could easily wriggle free.

"If they come down before I figure out how to get us out, I want them to think you're still passed out. So just lie there and don't move." She obliged, and in the dim light I wasn't sure whether she gave me a stink-eye.

I inspected the window first. It was boarded on the inside, and although our captors were stupid enough to use zip ties, they weren't so dumb as to leave crowbars lying around. I borrowed Suzi's gloves for protection while I stood on a filthy wooden bench and pried at the loose board. I got some leverage and it came off on the third yank. That was when I saw that the window was also boarded on the outside. It still seemed like the better escape route than up the stairs into…who knew what.

Getting the inside boards off was the easy part. The window itself was intact. I waited for the next rumble. Glad once again for the gloves, I broke the window under cover of the noise and picked out the glass. The heat from outside entered the damp basement.

Suzi had rolled over so she could watch me.

"Think about where we could be. It sounds like near an 'L' line," I stage-whispered to her.

I had just removed the first outside board, so there was enough light in the basement for me to see her smile.

"That doesn't narrow it down a lot," she whispered back. "There are a lot of 'L' lines."

The second board I pulled out was low in the window so I could see outside: we were in a neighborhood. A really poor neighborhood, with abandoned houses and rundown commercial buildings and broken sidewalks and weeds. The elevated train track ran down the middle of the street, and occasionally cars drove by.

Two more boards to go and there would be room for us to climb out. That's when I saw it: the dark sedan. It was coming toward the building but turned onto a side street before passing in front of us.

"Shit."

Suzi replied with an alarmed "What?"

"That car. It just turned, like it's going into an alley. I saw the same car this morning in your neighborhood. Can you get yourself up? We need to get out of here fast."

With the two of us pushing, the last two boards popped out. I used my suit jacket to cover the remaining shards of glass as we climbed to the sidewalk. Suzi was light; I was able to push her up enough that she could pull herself through and out to the sidewalk. She helped pull me up and I cleared the window just as I heard noise beyond the basement door.

We started running in the direction opposite from where the sedan had come. I could hear a voice behind us, shouting through the broken window. I couldn't understand his words but they sounded Russian.

We ran past a series of buildings like the one we'd climbed out of: three- and four-story red brick apartment buildings, most of them boarded. The shadow from the "L" track added to the twilight. I had no idea where we were going. We'd made it a block before I heard the shouting again, this time from outside. I heard footsteps but didn't take the time to turn back so I wasn't even sure how many guys were chasing us. It sounded like two.

A few cars drove by. Nobody stopped. A block ahead of us at the corner were four young men hanging out. They watched us being chased toward them. As we approached I could see them looking at us and laughing. The shortest of the men said something to his friends and shouted at us.

"Turn the corner! Go that way!" He pointed us left at the side street.

Normally I don't follow the advice of strangers but putting a corner between us and the Russians seemed like a good idea. At least they wouldn't be able to see us—or shoot at us—for a minute.

"Do it," I yelled at Suzi, and she turned left, with me two steps behind her. As we passed them, the other three men closed ranks, blocking the sidewalk after us. The short one ran with us and pointed to a small store a half-block ahead.

"Get in there!" He followed us into a liquor store where virtually all the product was behind Plexiglas panels, along with the clerk, who barely looked up at us from his cell phone.

"Let 'em in," the short man instructed the clerk, who did as he was told. The short man ushered us through a locked employee entrance into the secured booth behind the Plexiglas windows. He pushed us under the counter where we couldn't be seen from the street, and he ducked, too. We waited there about ten seconds.

"They gone," said the clerk as the Russians ran by the store.

"Fuckin' Russians," said the short man as he helped us up. "This is our fuckin' neighborhood." Then he stopped and looked at us, especially Suzi, who managed to maintain the hot middle-aged suburban housewife vibe despite all day on a basement floor and a three-block sprint in summer heat.

"Whatcha doin' with them?" he asked.

I had to laugh, maybe out of relief. "Doing with them? We weren't doing anything. They kidnapped us. We've been in their basement since this morning. Luckily whoever boarded that window wasn't much of a carpenter." The oddness of the situation suddenly dawned on me. "Why did you help us?"

"I told you. Fuckin' Russians. Got no fuckin' business in this neighborhood. Kidnapping people. This be our neighborhood. If anybody's gonna be doing any kidnapping, it's us." He laughed. I hoped he was joking about the kidnapping part.

His friends walked into the liquor store, and the euphoria from escaping the Russians quickly wore off. Two of them were looking through the glass at Suzi like she was prime rib at Lawry's.

"So, are you? Kidnappers, I mean." I tried to smile and keep it light, but the short man could tell I was faking it. He laughed.

"No, lady, that's not our style. But if you need any weed, I can hook you up." He laughed again when I smiled and shook my head "no, thanks."

"What's your recommendation for getting out of here, away from these guys?" Other than no car, no phone, no money, and at least two pissed-off Russians after us, we were in great shape.

The short man opened the door and nodded at one of his friends to come back. They spoke quietly for a minute, and in a strong enough street dialect that I had no idea what they were saying.

"Marcel here," the short man introduced his friend. "Marcel here'll get you over to the 'L' station. Give us ten minutes." He grinned. "We're gonna create a distraction."

"I really don't know how to thank you," Suzi said.

Marcel gave her a look that provided a clear and specific answer, but the short man slapped him on the side of his head.

"Marcel's gonna take you to the 'L' station," he repeated slowly, for Marcel's benefit rather than for ours. "And that's all. Right, Marcel?"

Marcel nodded but looked disappointed.

"Remember: ten minutes. Then get to the Cicero station and stay out of sight until the train comes. Then head downtown."

I dug into my pocket and pulled out air. "We don't have any money for the train. Maybe we could use your phone and call somebody? They could come get us."

"You don't want to wait around here that long," said the short man. I couldn't argue. He stepped in front of the clerk, opened the cash drawer, and pulled out a five. The clerk acted like this happened all the time.

"That'll get you to the Loop," he said, and walked out with his other friends.

The next ten minutes passed very slowly. The store was small; the only inventory not behind the locked counter were bags of chips in metal racks and a cooler of soft drinks. I chattered like an idiot, trying to distract Marcel from Suzi. I succeeded in annoying everyone, which was better than the alternative scenarios I was imagining. Suzi was very focused on the clock, and at exactly ten minutes she cried, "Time!" Then we heard the explosion. As we left the store and headed around the corner to Cicero, we could smell smoke. The sirens began.

"Damn fools," Marcel muttered as we jogged to the station. "Blowin' shit up so close to the train. You ladies get on that train and don't get off until Randolph Street. They're probably gonna shut the Green Line down 'cuz of this fire, so you get downtown and then find some nice person to get you home."

19

Detective Logan parked a couple blocks away from the South Paulina address he had jotted in his notebook. The sun was no longer high, but it was still powerful. He deferred to the heat by leaving his suit jacket in the back seat of his Ford, but kept his tie on. Younger people were more informal, but he liked being old school, dressing like a professional.

A utility van was parked around the corner from the two-story red brick apartment building that was Nooky's current address. Logan knocked on the back door of the van and was granted entrance, which meant the help of two officers pulling him up the steep step. The air conditioning was welcome after even a three-minute walk in this weather. From the monitors inside he observed the scene. There was a young African-American woman sitting on the porch of a boarded house across the street from the building, having a smoke. She stared vacantly but her eyes often lingered on the red brick building. Two middle-aged men, one Latino and one white, both disheveled, walked up the sidewalk near the building, stopping occasionally to argue. They pushed a rusted grocery cart filled with the debris of unhappy lives.

A silver sedan crept by, its rear windows rolled down. From the angle of the cameras Logan could not see the face of the person who stuck an automatic pistol out the window and fired at the red brick building.

The shots occurred at the same time the smoking woman stood up and the disheveled men snapped into action. All three individuals donned helmets and pulled out weapons. From the side of the boarded house a SWAT team appeared. The woman shattered the silver sedan's windshield with two shots. The men dove behind some garbage cans which had been conveniently placed near the street and filled with sand. From behind the cans, they joined the SWAT team firing at the car. In thirty seconds, it was over.

Logan carefully climbed out of the van. He wasn't worried about bullets anymore, but rather his dignity in hopping from the last step to the street. He needn't have worried; the operation he architected had been graceful enough that his physical bearing was forgotten.

The woman from the porch removed her helmet as she sprinted down the street to Logan. "We got him. Shot in the arm, but alive."

"The others?"

"Two other guys in the car. One dead, and one wounded. I've got EMT's on the way. We'll get Jones bandaged up and take him in tonight."

"Nice work, Sergeant," said Logan. "Very nice work."

The woman grinned. "Nice trap," she replied.

"I can hardly wait to call the task force." He had a spring in his step as he walked back to the sedan.

Logan didn't mind his microwaved dinner that night. Didn't mind it at all.

20

Marcel had been right: we were on the last "L" train that would be running for a while. Just like he told us, we got off at Randolph. There was a high end coffee shop nearby, and we persuaded one of the baristas to let us use their phone. I called Bill's cell.

"Where are you? Are you all right?" Bill's voice had the forced calm tone he'd learned from his military experience, working under fire.

"Fine. Safe, but stranded downtown. What happened? Are you and Stendahl okay?"

"Yes, although he's frantic. They grabbed me first, then him, and blindfolded us and tied us up, but left us fine. They were just buying time to get you away. There were three of them. They left us a ransom note, along with the usual, 'don't call the cops.' We were able to get out shortly after they drove off with you and Mrs. Stendahl. Charlie and I have been working all day trying to figure out where they might have taken you. A couple of hours ago Stendahl got a call that they wanted twenty million dollars for you. Well, for Suzi. Then we got an email with wire transfer instructions. Charlie wasn't able to track down the IP address. The drop was supposed to be at nine tonight, after the wire transfer."

"But he didn't send the money yet?" I hoped.

"No. Your timing is very good." Bill laughed, which made me laugh, which made Suzi smile.

"Let me talk with Bob," she said, grabbing for the phone. The barista appeared a little annoyed. I told Bill where we were, and handed Suzi the phone. "Make it quick."

She cooed for a moment, and the barista gave me a look. I nodded to him.

"Let's go," I said to Suzi.

She reluctantly returned the phone. "Bob's sending a car," she said. "It shouldn't be long."

We waited inside the coffee shop, despite the barista's glare. Standing on the street seemed too vulnerable. It was only a few minutes before the car arrived with Tom Donnelly in the back seat.

"I was parked at the construction office and Mr. Donnelly insisted on coming along," the driver explained. We packed into the car quickly and he pulled back into the slow-moving traffic.

"Are you ladies okay? My God, what happened?" Tom's hair had never looked so good.

Suzi, sitting between Tom and me, collapsed into tears while I reviewed the day.

"So the drug dealers rescued you?"

"I don't like to think of it that way. I got us out of the basement, after all. And I don't know that selling weed makes you a drug dealer, exactly."

Tom tried to climb out of the hole he had dug while I realized I was being a bit of a jerk.

"I didn't mean rescued, really," he said awkwardly. "I just meant that they helped hide you from the Russians."

"No, you're right. They did help rescue us." The absurdity of those events made me start to laugh.

Tom smiled. Suzi inquired at me through wet eyes.

"Well, it was pretty crazy. To have guys on the street save us," I admitted.

Tom began to laugh and Suzi finally smiled.

"I guess so," she admitted. "I'm glad they were there." She managed a laugh, then apparently considered the consequences had they not been there because she started to cry again. Tom put his arm around her as the driver pulled in front of a very expensive-looking Gold Coast hotel. This was to be our home until we could figure out what to do about the Russians.

As it turned out, Bob spent a thousand bucks for the suite unnecessarily. When the cops came by to interview us, they said our newfound friends on the West Side had done more than simply create a distraction. Vladimir Orlov and another Russian had returned to the house after their short search for us, and were badly burned in the explosion and fire. The officers weren't aware that there might have been a third man. By midnight, Charlie texted Bill to let him know the guy had boarded a late flight back to New York. For the moment, at least, we seemed to be done with the Russians.

21

After a year in the security business and having met a couple of detectives in Miami who weren't complete assholes, I had begun getting over my lifelong dislike of cops. But old habits die hard, and my initial response to a badge remained negative until proven otherwise.

So when a Detective James Logan showed up at the Stendahl Group Tuesday afternoon, bothering Alissa Marek, our receptionist, and demanding to speak to Bob, it was natural for me to be suspicious. I was in front of the conference room where Bob was conducting a meeting when Alissa called me to the front.

"What's this about?" I asked.

"I have some questions for Mr. Stendahl." Logan's face was damp; there seemed no end in sight to the heat wave.

"Mr. Stendahl is busy right now. Why don't I get your card and we can call you when he's free?"

"No, Miss…um, Miss…"

"Johnson," I supplied. "Tina Johnson. I handle security for Mr. Stendahl."

Logan looked a little surprised. This was not an uncommon reaction.

"Well, Miss Johnson, I have a matter of considerable importance and some urgency, so I would like to speak with him immediately." Logan straightened up and stared at me. His eyes were sharp and told me that judging this book by its sweaty, chubby cover would be a mistake.

"Are you here about the incident yesterday?" I escorted him behind the wall, out of Alissa's earshot. The staff hadn't been told about the kidnapping, and there was no reason to cause a panic among employees.

"You mean Orlov?" Logan confirmed that he wasn't an idiot.

I smiled. "Yes, sir. Mrs. Stendahl and I didn't get much of a look at them, but if there's anything we can help you with we're happy to. Obviously, we gave a full report to the officers last night."

"Obviously." Logan stared me in the eye. He pulled a notebook out of his jacket pocket but didn't open it. "No, this isn't about him. By the way, the two of them are going to be in the hospital for a while. Your friends pulled quite a stunt."

"They weren't my friends. They were just these guys on the street who got us out of the neighborhood. I certainly didn't ask them to blow up the house. Until we heard the noise, we didn't know what they were doing. I can't say I'm sorry that the Russians are in the hospital, but I'm glad no one else was hurt."

"Why do you think they helped you?" He still hadn't opened his notebook.

"Honestly? I think they thought it was funny. To see these white women running down the street, being chased by a couple of screaming Russians." I couldn't help smiling at how ridiculous we must have looked to them. "And I don't think they liked foreigners in their neighborhood."

"Probably not." Logan sighed. "But that isn't why I'm here. I need to talk with Robert Stendahl about a situation with a Ms. Krista Jordan and..." He finally flipped open his notebook. "A Mr. Stuart Mackenzie." He looked up at me. "Do you know either of them?"

"I met Mackenzie."

Logan waited. I almost thought he was counting to himself. We were mid-standoff when a door down the hallway opened. Several people came out and filed past us. Bob was not among them.

"Is Mr. Stendahl in there?" Logan took a few steps toward the conference room, and I tried to run in front of him.

"I don't know Mr. Stendahl's schedule," I lied. "Let me check with him to see if he has some time now."

"Whether he has time or not, I'm going to talk with him," Logan's stride lengthened and he beat me to the open door. At the end of a long conference room table sat Bob, going over notes with his assistant.

"Mr. Stendahl, this gentleman is a police detective and would like to talk with you." That was enough for Stendahl to stand up and ask his secretary to leave. She shut the door behind her.

"Is this about yesterday? Have you arrested those criminals who kidnapped my wife?" He looked at me and realized he should add, "And Ms. Johnson here?"

"No sir, I'm here on another matter."

"He's here about Stu Mackenzie." Giving my principal a one-second notice in front of the police wasn't a very helpful heads-up, but it was the best I could manage given the circumstances. And apparently that was all that Bob needed. He didn't miss a beat.

"Mackenzie? That old man who was here a few days ago?"

"So you met him."

"Yes. He was here in the office. I think he was mentally ill or drunk. What day was that, Tina? We can check out front. It should be in the visitor log."

"What makes you say he was mentally ill or drunk?" Logan began taking notes.

"He was ranting. We put him in a meeting room and gave him a cup of coffee. I spoke with him because he insisted on it, but finally we had to ask him to leave. I can't spend time with every crazy person in this city." Bob's tone suggested that Detective Logan was personally responsible for an outbreak of mental illness in Chicago.

Logan ignored Bob's comment and continued the interview. "What was he ranting about?"

"I couldn't really tell. He kept insisting that he had to talk with Mr. Stendahl. I'm not sure which Mr. Stendahl he meant, me or my father. Tina, do you remember anything more?"

I shook my head. My job here was to follow my client's lead, not to provide the cops with more information.

"Why did you give him coffee?" asked Logan. "Why didn't you just send him away?"

"We felt sorry for him. Figured maybe he'd calm down and leave without any trouble."

"Did he?"

"Yes, actually, he did. Left on his own."

Logan glanced at me. I nodded to reinforce my client's statement, and was glad that this part of it, at least, was true.

"What about Krista Jordan?" Logan looked at Stendahl, then at me. I waited for Bob.

"Krista Jordan? The name doesn't ring a bell."

My face went flat from the lie. Bob had spoken with Jordan's former employees at a restaurant in my presence, and had mentioned her name to Suzi. Logan didn't respond.

After a few seconds of silence, Bob broke. "Why are you asking about these people? Is that Mackenzie fellow all right? What did he do?" There was something in Bob's tone I didn't like. He knew more than he was saying.

Logan heard it, too. "They're both dead, Mr. Stendahl."

Bob's expression did not change immediately, but then he spoke. His voice backpedaled. "You know, I have heard of Krista Jordan. She owned a traffic signal company. Competitor of ours, as a matter of fact. I saw in the paper that she was killed in a car accident. Downstate, wasn't it? Young woman," he said for my benefit. "Very sad. I'm sorry that I didn't connect with the name when you first mentioned it." Bob didn't look sorry, and Logan didn't look like he believed him. "What happened to Mackenzie?" asked Bob.

"Also a traffic collision," Logan said. "Hit-and-run."

"That's a shame." Bob spoke without emotion. He looked at Logan. Logan looked me. I looked at them both.

"Well, I've got to get to a conference call," said Bob, importantly picking up a stack of papers on the table in front of him.

"I have some more questions."

"Well, why don't you write those questions down and give them to Ms. Johnson. Then we'll get back to you."

I waited, curious for Logan's response.

"No sir, that isn't going to work. We know who killed them."

Nicely played, Detective. Bob looked up more quickly than he had surely meant to.

"Killed both of them? What a strange coincidence. Was Mackenzie killed downstate, too?" He asked the question in a hopeful tone.

"No sir. Mackenzie was killed in the city, but they were both killed by the same people: associates of Terrance Jones."

The blood drained from Bob's face. He looked down at his papers until he recovered. That took two full seconds. I watched Logan, who observed Bob without displaying any expression of his own.

"Jones? Thomas Jones?"

Logan appeared unimpressed with Bob's attempt to play dumb. "No sir, Terrance Jones. He controls a criminal organization in the city. I understand you know him."

Bob paused, looked above Logan as if he were trying to place the name, then looked the detective straight in the eye. "No, Detective. I don't believe I do."

"He believes that he knows you."

"Then he is mistaken." Bob's color had returned. "I don't know where I would have met someone like Mr. Jones." Bob picked up his cell phone from the table in front of him and started scrolling through email.

"He said something about your not paying him enough to take the fall himself."

Bob stiffened, his finger still, but he didn't look up from the small screen. "I don't know what that means, Officer."

"Detective."

"What?" Bob was able to return to scrolling. He refused Logan's eye contact.

"I'm a police detective, Mr. Stendahl. But the larger point is that Terrance Jones has stated that you paid him to have two individuals killed."

"He is wrong." Bob must have decided Logan was bluffing. He casually picked up a file. "Now, I do have that conference call."

Logan pulled his cell phone from his jacket pocket, punched a couple of buttons, and handed it to Bob. "Perhaps if you saw a picture of him."

Bob returned the phone to Logan after looking at it just long enough. "No, I don't know who that is," he said.

"Do you recognize him, Ms. Johnson?" Logan handed me the phone.

I looked at the headshot of a total stranger. Before he could stop me, I pulled up the details on the picture and saw it had been taken that day. Logan quickly grabbed his phone back.

"No, Detective. I don't recognize him."

Logan stared at me as I shook my head. He turned toward Bob.

"So, Mr. Stendahl, your statement is that you don't know Terrance Jones?"

"Yes, Detective. That is my statement. I'm not sure how I can be any clearer." Bob turned to leave the room.

Logan jotted something in his notebook and flipped it closed. "Then that's all I need. For now."

"Ms. Johnson will show you out," Bob said as he left through the rear door of the conference room. The door went into a back hallway that led only to a storage room, but Logan didn't know that.

Logan stopped as we walked to the front of the now empty room. He turned to me. "How long have you been working for Bob Stendahl?"

"A few weeks."

"You didn't recognize Terrance Jones?"

"No." I wanted to move toward the door, but Logan's considerable heft and a couple of chairs blocked me.

"Jones is a bad guy. And I can't believe you haven't seen him before. He runs drug activity on the South Side. There've been pictures of him in the *Tribune*, the *Sun-Times*." He looked at me.

I shrugged. "I'm not from Chicago. I live in Miami."

Logan seemed to find that interesting. He reopened his notebook and scribbled something. "So you were hired all the way from Miami to do protection work for the Stendahls."

I didn't like being questioned. "It would seem that way, wouldn't it?" I asked him.

"Are you working for Bob personally or for the company?"

"You'll need to ask my boss that, Detective. I don't see invoices."

Logan closed his book. Rather than being angered by my insolence, his curiosity seemed piqued.

"You ever been on the wrong side, Miss Johnson?"

"The wrong side of what?"

"The wrong side legally, morally. Ever have a client who was the bad guy rather than the good guy?" This was not a question I expected.

"No. What are you saying?"

"I'm saying that your client hired one of the most violent men in Chicago to kill two people. That makes him a bad guy, and a dangerous one at that. I'm saying that you'll have to figure out which side you're on."

Logan walked to the door and raised his hand without turning around as he stepped into the hallway. "I can see myself out."

22

I was still thinking over what Logan had said when Bill relieved me at seven. We stood in the Stendahls' entryway on a throw rug that would have paid my Miami rent for a month. Bob and Suzi were upstairs; Bob in his home office, and Suzi videoconferencing with a grandchild who lived in Denver.

"We had a visit from a Chicago Police detective this afternoon," I said.

Bill waited for more.

"He questioned Bob about the deaths of Stu Mackenzie and a woman named Krista Jordan. Mackenzie was the old man who came to the office last week. Jordan apparently owned a company that is a competitor of Stendahl's."

"Why does the CPD think Bob knows anything about this?" Bill was only partly asking a question. I found his tone odd.

"They were suspicious hit-and-runs, apparently. But the real reason is that some big criminal, Terrance Jones, is the guy who killed them, or had them killed, and somebody's saying that Stendahl paid Jones to do it."

Bill's normal poker face broke for a split second, but he didn't say anything.

"Stendahl denied everything," I continued. "The detective, James Logan, didn't believe him." I paused and dropped my voice. "I didn't, either."

Bill said loudly, "Let's check the front of the house." He led me outside and we walked to the middle of the driveway, twenty feet from the garage. He looked around before speaking again, this time in a voice not much louder than a whisper. "So what do you think is going on?"

I shrugged, dropping my voice to match his. "I don't know, but Stendahl clearly knows something. Remember last week when he ditched me to go to the construction office? I have no idea where he went. And of course I don't hear his conversations in the office. I don't know what goes on in there, who he's talking with on the phone."

Bill's eyes darted around us. He said nothing.

Finally, I broke. "What?" I asked. "What do you know?"

"I heard Bob on the phone. It was the night Mackenzie came to the office. I heard him say 'Terrance.'"

"What else did he say?"

"I couldn't hear. He made the call and then realized I was in the room, so he walked out and pulled the door behind him."

"He called from his cell?"

"He called from a cell, but not his normal one. He was secretive but didn't seem frightened, so I figured he was using a separate phone to have an affair."

"With a Terrance?"

Bill shrugged. "Whatever. It happens."

We both stared at the three-story house in front of us, as if the building could give us answers.

"The detective said something really interesting to me after Bob left the room today," I said. "He told me I was on the wrong side, that Stendahl was a dangerous and bad guy. You've been doing this longer than me. Have you ever had something like that happen before? When you were protecting the bad guy?"

"No." Bill shook his head. "The worst I've ever had was a cheating husband who didn't want me to tell his wife. I've certainly never had a principal, and a partner, be kidnapped. And I've never had a cop say something like that."

"What do you think?" In the months we had worked together, I had grown to value Bill's opinion a lot.

"I think Logan's right."

23

"Linda Patterson!" Logan's eyes lit up when he saw her enter the detective room of the First District station. "I haven't seen you in a hundred years! Not since I was doing patrol in Englewood and you were the glue that held the whole division together."

"It's been forever." Linda grinned. He allowed her to hug him as tightly as his large frame could accommodate. "And I think you know my niece, Angela Frank."

Logan saw Angela and looked surprised.

"Small world," Angela said, with a smile and a shrug.

"Small world indeed. I can't believe you never told me you had a niece, Linda. I thought we were closer than that." Logan's exaggerated pout made Linda laugh as he escorted them to his desk.

"You always were my favorite." Her smile changed from humor to something deeper. She put her hand on Angela's shoulder. "I just learned about Angela and her mother."

Logan's grin turned flat and he stared at Linda. "That's big news. And sorry, I didn't mean to make fun."

"You didn't know," she said, forgiving him with a slight shrug and a warm smile.

"Please sit down." Logan pulled up two ancient gunmetal gray chairs with dark green leatherette padding. The women sat, and Logan positioned himself in desk chair of a similar vintage. "Can I get you some coffee?"

Linda and Angela both shook their heads no. The trio sat awkwardly for a moment. Logan finally broke the silence.

"Are you here concerning Krista Jordan?"

"Yes, but we have something else we wanted to discuss as well," said Angela.

"Well, we are making progress in the Jordan investigation, but I'm not able to say more than that." Logan looked at Linda. "I'm sorry. You understand."

She nodded.

"The other matter has to do with our family history," Angela said, looking at her aunt. "Aunt Linda said you might be able to help with some information on a very old homicide."

Logan tilted his head slightly. "How old?"

"Nineteen forty-nine," said Linda. "The death of a bartender at the Hi-Di-Ho Lounge in Uptown."

"Nineteen forty-nine?" Logan grinned. "That was a little before my time." The women didn't return the smile, and he cleared his throat. "What is it that you want to know?"

Angela pulled some sheets of paper from her purse.

"The victim's name was Johnny Wilson. The police suspected a man named Larry DeLuca, because he had robbed the bar a few years before and lived in the neighborhood. But he left Chicago before he could be arrested, so the case was never solved." Angela stopped when she saw that Logan wasn't taking notes. "Here," she offered the papers to the detective. "I found this from old *Tribs*."

Logan allowed the papers to be set in front of him but he didn't look at them. "Why are you interested in a case that old? What is it that you want to know?"

"We found some other information." Linda stepped in. "The real killer was Floyd Stendahl."

Logan had been fidgeting with his pen, but at Linda's accusation he stopped cold and stared at her.

"Yes," she insisted. "*That* Floyd Stendahl."

"Okay, you've got my attention. What is this information that makes you think he killed a bartender…what, nearly seventy years ago?"

"A letter from my grandfather, Larry DeLuca," said Angela. "He wrote it to my grandmother, Aunt Linda's mother."

Logan squinted at Linda. "Does that mean Larry DeLuca was your father?"

Linda nodded.

"Okay," said Logan, setting his pen down. "You ladies are going to have to start at the beginning and I need a fresh cup of coffee."

24

I was not sorry when our second team, Miguel and Henry, arrived and I could go back to sleeping at the hotel. My guest room at the Stendahls' was more spacious than the hotel, and of course Suzi's food was better, but being back downtown gave me some privacy and, more importantly, time to think about what was happening.

My cell phone rang as I was putting on pajamas. It wasn't even nine o'clock, but it had been a long day and anyway, the most comfortable place in a hotel room is the bed.

"How's the Windy City?" asked Teresa when I answered.

"Hot," I said. "In more ways than one." I filled her in on the kidnapping and escape, and my concerns about the Stendahls.

"Your life is never boring," she said. "My big news is that I decided to get my house painted." Teresa lived in Jonesboro, Arkansas, where she worked for a bank she hated. As a black woman in corporate America, she'd hit the glass ceiling years ago. The limits she faced were made somewhat more palatable by the respectability of an impressive job title and good health insurance, but they still grated. Since we'd become millionaires, Teresa had talked about taking early retirement and moving somewhere, maybe even Miami, but couldn't seem to pull the plug. Old habits die hard.

"Getting ready to sell it, or are you going to stay?" We'd had this conversation before, and it always ended up with Teresa staying. I asked anyway, because it seemed like the sort of question a supportive friend should ask. I didn't want her to think I'd concluded she would never leave the bank.

"Oh, no decision yet, but it needs to be painted either way. I found a nice shade of deep green. It will look really different."

"It's already green," I said.

"This is prettier. Deeper."

I smiled and shook my head at what she considered change.

She seemed to hear my amusement. "It is," she insisted. "It'll be nicer. I'll send you a picture when it's done."

"That's something I don't miss about owning a home anymore," I said. "But do send me a picture." I was sitting on the bed and rearranged some pillows to get more comfortable. "Hey, Teresa, I need to talk through something with you. Stendahl is hiding something—probably a lot of somethings. There's no proof, and a lot of missing pieces so far, but I'm convinced he's involved in two deaths. At the least he's aware of what happened to the victims. This whole thing with Mason protecting the Stendahls has felt off from the beginning, but now it's getting weird."

"What does Bill think?" Teresa had never met Bill, but I'd talked about him enough that she understood my respect for him.

"Bill thinks Stendahl is up to something. He overheard him talking with the killer, right after Stu Mackenzie came to the office."

"Stu Mackenzie was the old man who was killed?"

"Yes, and the police think that Bob is involved."

"So what are you and Bill going to do?"

"That's my problem. Bill's position is that we've been hired to protect the Stendahls, and certainly they need protecting. If nothing else, Suzi is clearly at risk."

"Clearly."

"Bill and I talked about letting Charlie know, but as long as the checks keep coming Charlie won't care." I had imagined my conversation on this topic with Charlie a dozen times, and it always ended the same way, with Charlie telling me that I should do my job and stop asking questions.

"Why don't you quit? The three guys can take care of Suzi."

This was unexpected. "Really?" I asked. "You've always said I might as well stay with Mason. I sort of wanted you to tell me I shouldn't quit."

Teresa chuckled. "So am I that predictable?"

"Well, you're not what I'd call an impulsive person most of the time." I laughed. "But seriously, part of me wants to get far away from the Stendahls, and part of me thinks I should stick around."

"Because if you stick around, you'll be able to figure out what's happening."

We both laughed. "Yes, exactly. I guess I'm predictable, too." My phone buzzed. I looked at the screen—it was a Chicago area code with a number I didn't recognize. "Teresa, I've got a call that's probably work. I need to take it."

"Keep me posted," she said.

"I always do." In the moment it took to disconnect with Teresa, the other caller hung up. But I was curious who it was, so I called back.

"Hello?" The voice on the other end was male and a little cloudy.

"Someone just called this number."

The voice brightened with recognition. "Tina? Hi, sorry, it's Tom Donnelly. Hope I'm not bothering you."

"No, not at all. I actually have the night off."

"Yes, I thought so since your other guys were in town." He had thought this through. That was a little creepy, but I didn't say anything. "I was just calling to see, well, I had a dinner at Morton's, so I was in the neighborhood and thought that maybe we could, maybe, meet for a drink."

Visions of Tom's hair flashed through my head, but what I found most seductive about the invitation was the chance to see what Tom might tell me about his family's business after a couple of cocktails. And it sounded like he'd already made a good start.

"That would be nice," I said, trying to balance professional with friendly. "I'm staying on Michigan Avenue." I thought it discreet not to mention the hotel name, in case he mistook that for an invitation.

"I know."

That shook me for a minute even though I realized that of course he knew. His company was paying the bill—although, of course, he himself wasn't signing the check, so he would have had to ask someone. Again, slightly creepy, but my curiosity got the better of me.

"Would you like to go to the Signature Room in the Hancock Building?" he asked. "The view there is so much better than from that basement on the West Side."

I laughed but couldn't find a quick comeback, so I just said, "I need a little time. Shall I meet you there?"

"Why don't I pick you up in a cab in front of your hotel. Is a half-hour enough time?"

"Sure. The Marriott, but I guess you know that."

"Yes, I'll meet you on the Rush Street side. See you soon."

Touching up my makeup, I thought of Mark. We had met in New Orleans, the sex had been mind-blowing, and he helped me out when I got into a mess with a woman—a childhood friend—who'd stolen my identity. That mess led me to Florida and my job with Charlie. Mark had visited me there a few times, and I had been back to New Orleans twice to see him for long weekends. We talked every week or two, although his job as a computer science professor gave him more free time than mine did, so I was generally the one to disappear from our relationship. Other than the conversation when he told me the FBI was onto the Stendahls, we'd not spoken since I'd been in Chicago. We weren't exclusive, but I wasn't particularly interested in seeing anyone else and as far as I knew he felt the same way.

I stared in the bathroom mirror. My hair had needed a trim before I left Miami, and nearly three weeks in Chicago hadn't helped matters. I pulled it up with a clip that I thought looked reasonably sophisticated. It was easy to decide what to wear since I only had one dress with me: black, sleeveless, just above the knee and with a modest neckline. It was the kind that could be dressed up or down as the occasion demanded. Sometimes when you're providing personal security to wealthy people, a black pantsuit simply won't do. I considered a silver chain necklace, decided against it: this was an investigation, not a date. My black heels were low and I had to carry my shoulder bag for lack of a clutch, but all in all I looked pretty good. I stepped outside the Marriott just as Tom pulled up in a cab. For an investigation, not a date.

Tom jumped out and held the door for me. His eyes widened and he smiled.

"You look great!"

I think I blushed a little, because he looked pretty great himself, wearing a charcoal gray suit, with a blue and yellow tie loosened slightly at the collar. "Thanks. It's the only thing I brought with me that isn't a black pantsuit." I sat in the cab and he went to the other side to get in.

"You look pretty great in pants, too," he said.

I shifted in the seat, a little closer to the door.

He seemed to pick up on my discomfort. "Sorry. Maybe I shouldn't have said that."

"No, don't worry." I shook my head gently. "Always nice to get a compliment."

That put him more at ease, and he directed the driver. "Please drop us on the Chestnut side."

"You want I take Michigan or Rush?" asked the driver, not removing his earbuds.

"Michigan," Tom said firmly. "My friend is from out of town and I want to show her the sights."

The driver nodded, and slowly pulled out into the heavy Magnificent Mile traffic.

We lurched up Michigan Avenue, and it was well after ten by the time we'd traveled the seven blocks from the Marriott. Tom spent the trip pointing out landmarks like the old Allerton Hotel and the Water Tower. He handed the cabbie a twenty and held the door for me.

There was a line at the elevator, people waiting to see the city at night from the Hancock Observatory. The security guard recognized Tom.

"The Signature Room, sir?"

"Yes, please," said Tom as we were escorted past the tourists into a separate elevator. The guard pushed the button and we began our ninety-five-story ascent.

"I guess we don't look like tourists," I offered. "Or are you a regular?" As I spoke, I wasn't sure whether I'd overstepped, so I grinned, hoping he took it as a joke.

"It's not a good idea to be a regular at a bar where you've got a thousand-foot elevator drop on your way home. Not great if your head is spinning already." He laughed, and I was relieved that I hadn't offended him.

"I guess not. I'll bet the view is spectacular."

"It is. It's nice for lunch, because you can see for miles, but at night I think it's especially exciting. The lights are gorgeous. And even when it's foggy, the experience is unique. Most beautiful city on earth." He smiled. "As you can tell, I am madly in love with Chicago."

"It's quite a city," I said, sort of in agreement with him.

"You've not had a chance to experience the good parts yet," he said.

"No, although seeing the lake every morning on the drive in is a great way to start the day."

He nodded and we reached the ninety-fifth floor.

"By a window, please," he asked the hostess, who led us to a couple of comfortable leather chairs with a small table between them. The décor wasn't anything special, but it didn't need to be. I nearly gasped as I looked out the floor-to-ceiling windows.

"That's south," Tom said in a tone that managed to be both understated and proud at the same time. "And look over there." He pointed to the left. "That black nothingness is the lake."

We just stood there for a few minutes, the view pure black on one side and shiny city lights on the other. A thousand feet below us, specks of light moved along Michigan Avenue and Lake Shore Drive. Tom sat down and finally I joined him.

"Pretty cool, huh?" He grinned.

"It's certainly a better view than I had the other day," I admitted with a laugh.

The waitress appeared from behind and asked for our order.

"Do you like gin?" Tom leaned toward me a little. "They have a great Pimm's Cup."

"Sure," I said, embarrassed to admit that I had no idea what a Pimm's Cup was.

"Two," he said to the waitress, who nodded and walked away. "I think it's English," he said to me. "It has ginger beer in it. Sort of a strange combination of things, but it tastes good."

"Okay, thanks." I was grateful that he didn't talk down to me. Other than Charlie, mostly people didn't anymore, but I'd spent more than a few years with a husband who had, and old anxieties linger.

"I hope you like it. If you don't, feel free to get something else."

"Thanks. I'm sure it will be good." We both turned back toward the window and sat in silence.

"So have you always worked in the family business?" I thought that would be a friendly question, natural, but also get us started in a direction I wanted to head.

"Since college. Wow. Time flies." He shook his head and that beautiful brown hair, spiced with a touch of gray, caught a light. I fought the distraction.

"You grew up in Chicago?"

"I did. Well, in Lake Forest. That's north of the city a bit."

"And your mom is Floyd's sister?" I had picked that up somewhere.

"Yes. His little sister. She passed away a few years ago." Tom's face clouded. "Alzheimer's."

I shook my head in sympathy. "My mom is gone, too. That's tough."

It was my good luck that the waitress chose this moment to appear with our drinks. I didn't want the conversation to continue into my personal life, or even Tom's. This was an investigation of the Stendahl Group's history, and I wanted to stay on topic.

I took a drink of the Pimm's Cup. It was lemony with a touch of mint and packed a punch. I took a second sip and set it on the table between us.

"You don't like it?"

"No, it's delicious. But it's strong, and I haven't had much to eat. I'll just take it slow."

"Let's fix that." Tom waved the waitress back over and ordered some hummus and pita bread.

"It must be interesting to be in a family business, especially one as big as Stendahl." I've found that the best way to get a man to talk is to sound fascinated with his career. It's a tactic that's transparent to women, but has never failed me with a guy.

"Well, it's not such a big business." Tom pretended to be humble as he took a drink.

"Seems pretty big to me. How long have you run construction?"

Tom took another sip and stared at his glass. "Twenty-one years." He shook his gorgeous hair. "Crazy, right?" He looked at me and smiled.

"Like you said, time flies. It must be really interesting." I picked up my glass and smiled back.

"Sometimes." Tom turned to the window and stared at the twinkling skyline. I sipped and waited. Eventually he gave in to the silence. "I hadn't planned to work in the family business. When I was in college I studied construction engineering because I *didn't* want to work for my uncle. Stendahl just did street lights and traffic signals back then. Uncle Floyd built it up from one of the earliest electrical contractors in Chicago to focus on government work. So I went into private construction and worked for a small firm in DuPage County for a few years. That was in the seventies, and the Western Suburbs were growing fast." He finished his drink, never shifting his eyes from the window. "But my boss started speculating on real estate, and got caught in the recession in the early nineties."

Despite drinking slowly I was starting to feel the booze. I began pretending to sip, barely wetting my lips, waiting for Tom to continue. This time, he didn't.

"What happened?" I finally asked. Tom shook his head with a jolt and I realized he'd been lost in his thoughts.

"Uncle Floyd to the rescue," he said bitterly. "He came in and bought the company right before we were going to shut down. Got some equipment cheap, but mostly he wanted the real estate."

I wet my lips on the gin and gazed out the window. The waitress brought a small bowl of hummus and a few triangles of pita. Tom ordered another drink. I declined.

"Floyd ran the whole company until he retired. When Bob came on as president, he focused more on growing the technology side of the business, so he put me in charge of construction." Tom finished his beverage, but held onto the glass. "The construction division is more local, mostly in Chicago and the suburbs. It's not sexy and it's not going to grow fast, so Bob's not particularly interested in it. He likes the international piece." Tom turned to me with a smirk that was both bitter and sheepish at the same time. "I guess you know that already."

"Yeah, I've heard." I laughed as the waitress brought Tom another Pimm's Cup.

Tom immediately took a slug.

"Anything for you?" she asked me. I covered my glass, still a third full, and smiled at her as I shook my head "no."

"Have you guys had trouble like that before? With the Russians? Bob was really secretive when he hired us. Told Charlie he needed security but wouldn't say why."

"Of course he wouldn't say why, because then he'd have been admitting to breaking federal law. When you sell technology to a hostile foreign government and the deal goes so badly that they send in thugs as collectors, you can't get protection from more..." Tom paused to take a long drink. "...from more official sources of protection. But to answer your question, no, we haven't had trouble like that before. Not for a long time. Not like that."

"Then like what?" I asked, intrigued by his last comment.

Tom sat his glass on the table, then reconsidered and picked it up. "Bob plays hardball," he said. "He believes in winning, and he doesn't always follow the rules."

"Rules, or laws?"

"Either. Both. We've had some securities investigations. But Bob is smart, too, and they've never been able to prove enough to prosecute. He's learned his lesson, in a twisted sort of way. That's what got him into trouble with the Russians. He'd made commitments to investors that we'd hit certain sales targets, and by God, he made sure we did—even if it took breaking federal law by selling restricted technology to do it, and even if it meant promising the customer more than we could deliver." He shook his head and took a sip, followed by another, longer. I watched him, then peered into my glass as the last bit of ice disappeared.

"But he's never been involved in violence before, has he?" Maybe the Pimm's had gone to my head more than I'd thought; this was an amateur question. Tom, however, didn't seem to think the question was inappropriate.

"No. That was Floyd."

This was not the answer I was expecting. It didn't seem to be the answer Tom had intended to give, either. He glanced at me quickly, then returned his gaze to the city lights. Two more long sips. The ice clicked in his glass.

"Floyd? What happened?"

"Oh, that was a long time ago. I shouldn't have said anything."

We sat for a few minutes, me nursing my Pimm's, and him drinking his the way you drink water on a hot day.

"You can't just say something like that and not tell me the story." I tried to sound more playful than serious. It worked.

"It was a really long time ago. Back in the forties. Floyd…well, Floyd hurt someone."

I sipped my drink, a real sip this time.

"My mother was something of a free spirit, at least back then. She started dating a kid in Uptown, not far from her neighborhood but worlds apart, if you know what I mean. And Floyd didn't like the kid. He was a couple of years older than Mother, and worked in a bar. I think it was his dad's bar, but that didn't make any difference to Floyd. The kid wasn't good enough for his baby sister. Floyd apparently tried to convince Mother to break up with him but of course that didn't work. So one night Floyd gets in a fight with the guy…"

Tom had not turned his eyes from the window during the story. Now his voice drifted toward the skyline as well. I took a fake sip, then a real one.

"What happened to the boyfriend?" I spoke just above a whisper, because Tom seemed in a different world.

"He died." Tom shook himself out of his daze and looked at me. His tone sharpened. "Floyd killed him."

"In the fight?"

"Yes, but Mother told me that he had brought a knife to the bar. She thought that Floyd killed him on purpose. He came in on a weeknight, when hardly anyone would be there."

The waitress came by again, and I signaled for two more drinks. I didn't want Tom to stop talking for any reason.

"How long have you known this?" I leaned forward in my chair and tried to think what I'd do if I knew a family member murdered someone.

"Mother told me a few years ago. As she was starting to get sick." He took a last swig and set the empty glass on the table.

"Did you tell anyone?"

"I asked Floyd about it. He didn't deny it, exactly. He just told me nobody would believe an old lady with Alzheimer's. He actually called his baby sister 'an old lady with Alzheimer's.'" Tom shook his head, but this time I didn't notice his hair, only the reddening around his eyes.

I waited a moment to convey sympathy for the slight. I wasn't sure whether Tom was more upset that his uncle had knifed a man to death, or insulted his mother.

"So there weren't any witnesses? Besides your mother?"

"Mother hadn't actually seen it. She was upset when Floyd came in and left the bar before anything happened. But Mother said there was a couple sitting in the corner. I guess Floyd threatened them into keeping quiet."

"How?"

The waitress brought fresh drinks; Tom took a gulp and held the glass. I sipped mine and set it on the table. Tom just shook his head, and it wasn't clear whether he didn't know or simply couldn't say any more. We sat that way, looking out the floor-to-ceiling windows at Chicago's lights, for a long time. If Stu Mackenzie had witnessed the killing and was trying to blackmail Floyd, he'd waited an awfully long time to do so. I rolled that around in my mind and swirled the remains of the Pimm's Cup. Tom waited for me to finish my drink before he spoke.

"Ready?" His tone was back to normal, as if nothing had happened. "Would you like me to walk you back to the hotel? I could use some air."

25

I was in Mark's arms, warm in bed at home. When the alarm went off, it sounded different. Groggy, I saw that rather than coming from the side of the bed with the clock, which read 2:00 a.m., and rather than the bed being in my apartment in Miami, the alarm was actually my cell phone buzzing and the bed was in a hotel room in Chicago. Rolling over to pick it up cleared my head from thoughts of Mark. The voice on the phone took care of any fog that was left.

"Tina? *Jesus*, get out here." Even through the last bit of fog I recognized Miguel's voice. Perfectly neutral American accent, except when he was stressed and reverted to his parents' *Cubano*.

"What's wrong?" I sat up and was glad that I'd not ordered a third drink.

"Bill's dead. Shot."

"Where? At Stendahl's? What the hell happened?" I held the phone with my shoulder and pulled on a pair of black pants. Bill dead? I knew Miguel wouldn't make a joke about this, but I couldn't think of another reason why he would say it. Bill couldn't be dead.

"Yes. Two guys in the back yard, I guess trying to break in. We got one of them, but there was another who took off. I've called the police."

"I'm on my way," I said, pulling the pajama top off over my head and the phone. "Not sure how long it will take, but I'll get there as soon as I can." So far I'd had a car service take me back and forth to the Stendahls, or else Bob's personal driver. Neither seemed feasible at two in the morning. I had no idea what a taxi would cost, but I didn't think either Charlie or the Stendahls would balk at the bill.

Even at such a late hour on a weeknight, it took the doorman no more than a minute to scare up a cab. We drove north on streets that were deserted by Chicago standards and got to the Stendahls' home in just over thirty minutes.

Their street was filled with emergency response vehicles, lights flashing. I wondered whether the five squad cars, two fire trucks and two ambulances comprised the entire public safety fleet of the wealthy village. Miguel stood in the front yard. Two paramedics pushed a stretcher with a sheet-covered body down the driveway, already full of vehicles, and I had to join Miguel in the grass to get out of their way. The tension in my stomach, building since the wake-up call, nearly erupted. I pressed my eyes closed and took a breath, only opening them when I felt Miguel's hand on my shoulder.

"That's the other guy," he said, which didn't make me feel any better. "Bill is already in there." He nodded toward one of the ambulances.

My brain shifted to work mode. "That was fast."

We were joined by Henry, a six-foot former Florida State linebacker whose head ran into his massive torso with no apparent neck. "Yeah. They don't waste any time getting things tidied up out here."

"What happened?"

"We were in the kitchen," Henry nodded toward Miguel, "and Bill was doing a perimeter around the yard. The principals were both in their bedroom."

"Quiet," added Miguel.

"Yeah, it was quiet. Bill only went outside out of habit. You know Bill, always a stickler for procedure."

I smiled grimly at that. Whenever we had an indoor team who could closely protect our principals, Bill liked to do outdoor patrol several times a night, although never on a predictable schedule. My smile faded as the reality hit me again.

"Bill was in the back yard when we heard noise from that direction. Miguel went upstairs to cover the Stendahls and I opened to patio door. I hadn't even gotten outside when I heard three shots." He paused and looked at Miguel.

"Yes, three shots." Miguel nodded to confirm.

"I saw Bill fall," Henry continued, "and another guy, and then a second man ran off. He ran toward the back yard of that blue house next door, so I couldn't fire. It was all over in less than five seconds."

"Who were they? More Russians?"

Henry snorted. "Black Russians, maybe."

"The shooter was black," explained Miguel.

"And the other guy?"

"It was too dark to tell," Henry said.

"No, I mean where did he go?"

"I couldn't see him once he got past the blue house. The police looked for him but I haven't heard how that ended. If they found him, they haven't told the guys on the scene here."

"And the Stendahls?"

"They're fine." Miguel sighed with some bitterness. "I woke them up, actually."

"I should check on Suzi," I said. I started toward the front door and realized I hadn't asked the name of the man who killed my friend. Before going inside, I closed my eyes and told Bill I would find out—not only the name, but why, and make sure that somebody paid.

26

Logan began his Thursday spending an hour with a dental hygienist who insisted that cell phones be turned off. When he arrived at the station around ten, torn between the desire to keep that shiny clean-teeth feeling and the need for coffee, he found a yellow Post-it on his chair. "See me," it said, written in his boss's heavy block hand.

The lieutenant growled at him when Logan popped his head inside the glass-walled office.

"Jones is dead."

"Dead? They told me at the scene that he'd be fine. It was just an arm wound. They fixed him up at the hospital and sent him to Cook County jail that night."

"That was two days ago. A lifetime, as it turns out, for Terrance Jones." The lieutenant fancied himself to be clever with words. Logan had learned to smile and say nothing. "Jones was released on bond yesterday morning."

"What?" Logan forgot about how good his teeth felt. "Who the hell ordered that?"

The lieutenant shook his head. "I know, I know. Between the hospital and Cook County, some idiot screwed up the paperwork. They released him Tuesday."

Logan swore silently, then out loud. Then he remembered what had started this conversation. "So how's he dead?"

"Killed in an attempted home invasion, on the North Shore." Papers shuffled as the lieutenant paused, and Logan waited. "Seems a bit far afield for our Mr. Jones, but there you have it." He handed a sheet to Logan.

"Doesn't make any sense. What's he doing all the way up there? And a home invasion? That's not his style." Logan studied the paper, then grinned with recognition. His boss grinned back.

"Yeah, I know. Small world, isn't it? Look, the boys up there, they just want to keep their wealthy citizens happy. They've decided it was an attempted home invasion, with the second perp having fled their jurisdiction and therefore their concern. They're sorry about the unfortunate loss of life of a security guard, but these things happen. He was hired help. Occupational hazard, they say. So they're done investigating."

Logan stopped smiling. "Security guard?"

"Yeah, William Bauer. Worked for Stendahl." The lieutenant paused to consider Logan's possible feelings in the matter. "Had you met him?"

"No," said Logan. He decided not to mention the woman bodyguard he'd spoken with. No need to make connections that the lieutenant might have to lie about later. This was not a CPD case. Logan wasn't sure what, if anything, he was going to do about it, but the less his boss knew, the better.

They stared at each other for what seemed a long time.

"I'd like to know why the hell Terrance Jones was at Bob Stendahl's house in the middle of the night," Logan finally said. His voice turned official. "Too bad CPD doesn't have any authority to investigate two homicides on the North Shore."

"Right, it's too bad," the lieutenant agreed.

"Well, I guess CPD is off the Terrance Jones case," Logan said, loudly enough that an officer passing by the open office door could hear. Logan made a mental note of the officer's name. It never hurt to have a witness.

"I guess we are," said his boss, equally loudly. He announced the meeting's conclusion by sitting down and directing his attention to his computer screen.

Logan flipped through his notebook as he walked back to his desk. Hadn't he gotten Tina Johnson's cell number? It was her buddy who'd been killed—hell, maybe they'd been more than buddies—and it seemed like a good time to check in. He was starting to curse his carelessness in not getting her number when the phone buzzed. Not an area code he recognized.

"Logan," he barked. When he heard the voice on the other end, he smiled and opened his notebook to a blank page. He decided he'd pick up a lottery ticket on the way home: this was his lucky week.

27

Henry had stayed at the house with Suzi, and Miguel had accompanied Bob to work that morning. I rode into town with them so I could check out of the hotel. We were all moving back to the house. Packing would only require five minutes, but I needed more time than that. I took a shower, the hot water mixing with memories of Bill. My big brother had taken off a few years ago, after our mother had died. In Bill I'd found a man to take his place: a true friend without complications, and now he was gone.

I sat at the desk in a towel and called Mark, for whom my feelings were anything but sisterly. He hadn't ever met Bill, but knew of our friendship and listened with sympathy when I told him what had happened.

"What's going on up there?"

"I'm not completely sure. Stendahl is involved in a lot. Two people were killed by a drug lord named Terrance Jones, and the police think that Bob was involved. Bill thought so, too." I shut my eyes and took a breath. Mark waited. "Presumably Bob hired Jones, but that isn't entirely clear. I don't know whether the cops heard that from Jones or another witness. And Floyd Stendahl, the father, killed a guy almost seventy years ago. One of the current homicides, one that the cops believe Jones did, was a man named Stu Mackenzie, who I think knew about the old murder. He came to the office a couple of weeks ago. I'm not sure how the pieces fit. Can you do some digging online for me, as long as you stay away from the Stendahls?"

"Of course. What do you want to know?"

That's just the kind of guy Mark is. I gave him the few details I knew and a list of questions I'd been pulling together in my head. He didn't flinch, at least not that I could tell over the phone, when I told him my timeframe. I got dressed, then dug around in my purse until I found Detective Logan's business card. I dialed and he picked up on the second ring.

"Logan." The detective's voice was louder than I recalled.

"This is Tina Johnson, Detective. We met at Bob Stendahl's office."

"Yes, I remember." He paused for a moment. "I'm sorry about your partner," he said. Bad news travels fast among law enforcement, apparently. I couldn't tell whether he was being polite or just trying to play me.

"Thank you. So you've heard."

"Yes." Logan paused, and when he spoke his voice stayed quiet. "Did they tell you the name of the dead guy?"

"No. They didn't tell us anything."

"Terrance Jones."

I took a step back and sat on the bed.

"Terrance Jones, the guy you think killed Stu Mackenzie and the woman? *That* Terrance Jones?"

"Yeah," Logan said dryly. "*That* Terrance Jones."

"I figured it was some kind of attempted robbery." My brain felt like a kaleidoscope, with tiny pieces of information rearranging themselves so quickly that I couldn't tell what any of them were.

"That was the official line. But suburban home invasion isn't really Jones' gig."

"And if it were he wouldn't be robbing someone he knew, right? So what the hell was he doing at the Stendahls' last night?" I turned the kaleidoscope more slowly, considering each piece. Floyd Stendahl killing his sister's boyfriend nearly seventy years ago. Stu Mackenzie threatening to go to the police about it. Bob Stendahl talking with Jones, then Jones sneaking through the Stendahls' back yard.

"That's a good question," said Logan. "Another good question is why he was even out of jail. Somebody at Cook County fucked up the paperwork and they let his girlfriend bail him out. I don't know whether that was incompetence by itself or whether somebody helped the incompetence along. I'd say it's even money either way."

More questions. This wasn't helpful. "I don't have a lot of time before I have to get back to covering Bob," I said. "Can we stop with the questions and get to what we know?"

"You go first." I could hear a thin smile in Logan's voice which reminded me that he was a cop.

"Bill heard Bob Stendahl talking with Terrance Jones on the phone, the night that Mackenzie had come into the office."

Logan waited. When I said nothing, he laughed. "So we're going to play tit for tat? That's not how it works. You tell me everything you know, because I'm a cop. That's how we do it in Chicago."

"But there are two deaths that aren't in Chicago, and you're not going to get very far with the local PD who seem happy to take the easy explanation. And while I don't expect you to care much that one of the deaths was of my friend, I think you care very much about the other one, since he was a key to your murders. A key, or a loose end."

"I've thought about whether Stendahl or Jones was the loose end here," Logan said, dropping his tough cop routine. "And I don't know who was which. Maybe Jones decided to kill Stendahl to clean things up, and was coming to the house for that reason."

"Why would Jones do that if he'd already given up Bob?"

"Fair point," mused Logan. "Jones isn't the kind of guy who normally cooperates with the police, but we caught him attempting to kill one of his guys who had killed Jordan and Mackenzie, and I think he decided he wasn't going to take the fall alone."

"So maybe Jones was targeted by Bob, out of revenge or simply to prevent him from testifying?" I asked.

"If Stendahl felt Jones was a loose end, Stendahl might have told him to come through the yard with the thought that you guys would assume it was a break-in and kill Jones," Logan said. "And as it turns out, that's what happened."

"But it was no secret that we were protecting the house. The way you described Jones, surely he would have been smart enough to figure that out. I don't see him letting Bob set him up like that. I mean, I don't see why Jones would have come to the Stendahls' home at all. He certainly wouldn't have tried to kill Bob at home with us there—why take that risk when it would be easier to get him somewhere else? And like we said, why would Jones need to kill Bob after already giving him to you guys? If he and Bob just needed to talk in person, they could find a better place than a house with a 24-hour security detail." I stood up and walked to the window, looking absently down at Michigan Avenue. The kaleidoscope in my head kept turning. Lots of pieces but nothing fitting together. "No," I said. "I just can't think of any set of circumstances where Jones would be sneaking around the back yard."

"It doesn't make sense," Logan agreed.

Suddenly the kaleidoscope came to a stop. "No, I'm wrong. There is one circumstance where Jones would be sneaking in the back way: he was there to kill us. To kill Bill. We were the loose ends." I choked for a minute. Logan's silence now felt like something approaching compassion. "So Stendahl and Jones plan this together: Stendahl knew that Bill had overheard him on the phone. He knew where Bill would be, which is at the house. Jones sets up a situation that looks like a threat to our client, and Bill does what Bill always did: protect the client. Jones simply had to wait for him to come outside and he'd be easy to get. Only Jones didn't count on Bill being such a good shot."

"And from Stendahl's point of view, it was a lucky break. Getting rid of Terrance Jones was a bonus." Logan's voice had dropped so much that I was barely able to make out his words. "Just a minute," he mumbled, and I wasn't certain whether he was talking to me or someone else. Then I heard traffic noise in the background on his end of the line, and his voice came back stronger. "Sorry, I had to step outside. Look, Jones was the prime suspect in two Chicago murders, and now Jones is dead. I've been told we're done. This is not a CPD investigation."

"Then what is it?"

"Some might say it's a private investigation being carried out by a bodyguard with a grudge. Or with a reason to be concerned about her own safety."

"I may be a girl from Omaha, Detective Logan, but even I can tell when I'm being set up."

He laughed at that. "I said some might say. I didn't say I would say. But it's important that you understand what I can and can't do to help."

"Okay, tell me."

"I can tell you what I know. And I want to introduce you to someone."

28

True to his word, Mark emailed me a report by the time I had to go back on duty. He had begun using a new protocol, he called it, to make it harder for the FBI to trace his searches back to him. Still, I told him to play it safe and not go anywhere too illegal. Luckily, he didn't need to.

He gave me bios of Stu Mackenzie and Krista Jordan, along with a remarkably complete profile of Krista's company, which included the name of the young woman Logan told me I should meet. That and some other information he provided started to pull a few things together in my head, but I wasn't able to do anything with his report for several days—not until after Bill's parents and Charlie came to Chicago.

Mr. and Mrs. Bauer came to escort Bill's body back to their hometown in the Florida panhandle. At first I assumed Charlie's mission was to support them, and us, and that after the murder of one of his employees he would be interested in the information I'd uncovered.

That was a stupid assumption. Charlie's primary concern was making sure that Bill's inconvenient death wasn't going to lose us the account. When I told him my theory, and the evidence that was starting to back it up, he immediately ended the conversation and avoided being alone with me for two days so I couldn't bring it up again. Finally, Saturday evening, I decided to play the woman card. I told him that I needed a day off after everything that had happened, and that Henry and Miguel would be able to handle the Stendahls on a Sunday. Which, of course, I did and they could, but that wasn't the reason I needed time away.

Charlie agreed I could take twenty-four hours off and rejoin the detail at Stendahl's office Monday morning. Stendahl's driver took us both to O'Hare: Charlie to catch an early Sunday morning flight and me to pick up a rental car. Charlie's last comment to me was "Your hotel tonight is on your own."

Obviously, I hadn't expected the company to pick up the hotel tab for my night off, but Charlie's attitude didn't improve my rapidly waning interest in Mason Security.

Logan had given me the number for Angela Frank, which I dialed as I sat in the rental car lot. A groggy voice answered, but brightened when I gave my name. I looked at my watch: not quite 8 a.m.

"Sorry it's so early," I said. "I only have today free and I need to make the most of it. Is there any chance I could meet you for coffee somewhere?"

"Detective Logan said you would be calling. He said you'd want to meet my Aunt Linda, too."

We discussed logistics: I would pick up Angela then swing south of downtown toward a place nearer her aunt's neighborhood. Traffic was light and I made it to Angela's apartment in twenty-five minutes. Beautiful old brick and stone buildings, tree-lined streets, and no available parking. I pulled as far as I could toward the vehicles parallel parked at the curb, but still blocked the narrow street. The morning air was balmy, not yet hot, and I opened the windows.

"Tina, right? Nice to meet you." A young woman leaned into the car to shake my hand, then jumped in. "I'm Angela. Thanks for picking me up."

"Of course. This gives us some time to talk."

Twenty minutes in the car with a stranger, however, doesn't give you a lot of time to talk, especially when the stranger is your navigator. So by the time we parked a half-block away from the South State Street coffee shop where we were meeting Angela's aunt, I hadn't learned much. Angela told me the circumstances under which she'd found Linda Patterson, including Stu Mackenzie's role, and I told her about Stu's argument with Bob Stendahl.

"So that's what he did!" Angela stepped out onto the curb and slammed the door. "That crazy old man, I never should have shown him the letter."

"What letter?" I asked as I shut the door, just in time to avoid a bicyclist zipping down the street.

"A letter that Aunt Linda had from my Grandfather Larry, my mom's birth dad. He had written it to my grandmother and it talked about what happened that night in the bar."

"So that's how Stu knew what happened." I wondered where the letter was.

Angela held the door of the coffee shop open for me and her eyes started to darken. "I should have known better than to let him see it, but he was so curious. He'd reunited Linda and me, so letting him look was a kind of thank you."

Before I could reply Angela ran to a light-skinned African American woman, older than me, who stood up from a table where she'd been drinking coffee and, apparently, watching the door. The women embraced.

"This is Linda Patterson," Angela said as she released her aunt. "Aunt Linda, this is Tina Johnson. It was her friend who was killed at the Stendahls'. She's been their bodyguard."

Linda's back stiffened and her mouth pursed. "You work for the Stendahls?"

"Yes, but that began before I knew anything about them."

Linda's posture loosened a bit, but she didn't sit down.

"I've spoken with Detective Logan," I said.

Her mouth became more neutral, although still nothing like a smile.

"The investigation into my partner's death is basically closed, and I think the Stendahls are responsible. I want to hold them accountable."

At this, Linda nodded and took a seat. "You girls get some coffee. And how about some of those almond croissants they have in the case. We have a lot to talk about."

29

Detective Logan had his doubts. When he had connected his old friend Linda Patterson and her niece to the woman bodyguard, his intention was not to get involved in a sting concerning a decades-old homicide. Certainly not a sting involving the fabricated story of an elderly would-be mobster returning from more than sixty-five years of exile in Mexico. Then again, he told himself, what else did he expect? These women were all determined, and a cop couldn't go after someone like Bob or Floyd Stendahl directly. They came up with this plan for lack of a better option, and he had nobody but himself to blame for the fact he was sitting in the cramped office—more like a closet with a desk, really—of a decrepit bar in Uptown.

It wasn't the Hi-Di-Ho. That building was long gone, cleared for a high rise in the late sixties. The bar where Logan sat wasn't vintage enough to appeal to hipsters like some of the places on Sheridan Road. It didn't seem to appeal to anyone except the two morning drinkers whom Linda had convinced to move down the street with some smooth words and a couple of six-packs. Their seats, one at each end of the bar, were filled by the same two cops who had been the homeless passers-by during the takedown of Terrance Jones not two weeks earlier. *Typecast,* Logan smiled to himself. The bartender was the cop who had sat on the stoop across the street. She had earned herself the role of tactical lead based largely on the fact that she didn't look disheveled enough to be convincing as a drunk.

Logan wasn't sure what to expect from the Stendahls, if they showed at all, but prudence seemed in order. The real bartender, a college student with dreadlocks and horn-rimmed glasses, was perched nervously on the desk, looking at his hands. Just to be safe, Logan had taken the kid's cell phone, and the kid knew better than to argue with a Chicago cop. Now the two men waited in silence.

"Angela and the old man are in position," said the woman's voice in Logan's ear. The bartender.

This was the part that made Logan the most uncomfortable. He didn't like the idea of using an old man, some neighbor of Angela Frank who was trying to avenge his friend's death, as bait. But when the bodyguard had asked him for a better idea, he hadn't had one.

Logan looked at the laptop in front of him. The view on the screen, coming through a button hole on Lester B. Moore's best collar shirt, was the door of the bar. His view shook a little.

"Tell him not to move around so much," Logan growled into his headset.

"Sir, try to stay still," said the tac leader to the old man. "You're jiggling the camera."

"It's going to be fine, Les." Angela's arm appeared on the screen as she reached up to pat Lester on the shoulder. The camera angle turned toward her as she shifted back into her seat next to the old man, then turned steadily back to face the door.

"Can you hear us okay?" Angela asked Logan.

"Yeah, fine. Just tell him not to move fast."

The tac leader brought club soda to Angela and Les, and returned to the bar just as Logan's screen flashed with glare. He blinked. The light quickly shrank as the door closed behind Floyd Stendahl, accompanied by Tina Johnson. Logan watched them look at the bar as their eyes adjusted to the darkness, then settle on the odd couple against the back wall. Stendahl was dressed in a light blue seersucker suit, befitting the season. He moved into the foreground of Logan's screen, glowering at Les. Tina stayed a few steps behind. No one spoke and for a second Logan worried that he'd lost sound.

"You the one that called me?" Stendahl had broken first. Logan smiled at the screen. They had told Moore to count to ten before saying anything, to make Stendahl uncomfortable with the silence, to make him the one talking. So far, so good.

"Yeah. I'm a friend of Larry DeLuca." Moore spoke evenly, just like they had practiced: *Forget about the mics. Just talk naturally.*

Stendahl didn't respond. Logan lost his smile at the silence, and began his count.

"You remember Larry." Lester B. Moore only waited until three-one-hundred to speak, and his voice went up a little. Logan shook his head. So much for following instructions.

"No, I don't think I do," Stendahl replied.

"He remembers you."

"Does he? And just where does he think he remembers me from?"

Asshole. Logan shook his head at the pomposity in Stendahl's voice and the college student bartender did the same.

"The old neighborhood. Not this bar, but one not too different. The Hi-Di-Ho. He saw you there one night."

"I don't know who you're talking about. As far as I know, everybody from the old neighborhood is dead." Stendahl was staring at Les, his face impassive.

"Funny thing about Mexico," Les said.

Stendahl's eyes widened for a millisecond, then narrowed and his deadpan returned. "Mexico?" Logan was impressed that Stendahl's voice only cracked a little. He was a tough old man.

"Yeah, Mexico. It's dry there, ya know. I've heard that dry heat makes people live a long, long time." Logan rolled his eyes and the nervous college student covered his mouth to suppress a laugh. At least Moore's voice had returned to a normal pitch.

"What does that matter to me?" Stendahl asked, his tone hard, but not angry. No emotion.

"Larry loved the heat, but he decided it was time to come home."

Stendahl blinked and turned behind him toward his bodyguard. Tina had positioned herself facing the bar, her peripheral vision covering both the front door and her boss. She was moving her head slightly from side to side to take in both angles, and didn't appear to have heard anything. Stendahl returned his attention to Les and Angela.

"Why don't you let us talk, young lady?" Stendahl asked.

Logan's screen bobbed three times as Les nodded in agreement.

This might just work. Logan allowed himself a little hope.

"I'll be in the washroom," said Angela. Les turned toward her as she stood up.

"No, why don't you go outside." Stendahl wasn't asking.

"But I do need to use the washroom."

Logan saw Stendahl reach out to grab Angela's arm. In the background, he saw his tac lead bartender watching. Tina walked toward them.

"Everything okay, Mr. Stendahl?" Tina asked.

Stendahl dropped his hand. "Yeah. I just want some privacy to talk with this, um, gentleman. I'd like the girl to step outside."

"Miss, why don't we go outside for a minute and let them tal'k?" The bodyguard smoothly guided Angela by her elbow toward the front of the bar. Logan saw Angela crane her head toward her neighbor, worry in her face. "Don't worry, Miss," said Tina. "They'll be fine." A moment later, the blinding glare returned, then vanished. The window air conditioner in the small office was barely working, and Logan felt his undershirt getting damp.

"So, Mr. Moore, is that right? Moore?" Stendahl sat across from Les, never taking his eyes from the old man's face. Logan wasn't sure whether Stendahl's clenched jaw was simple hostility, or if there was some anxiety mixed in.

"Yes sir, Lester B. Moore."

"Why don't you tell me what the hell is going on." Stendahl dropped his voice to nearly a growl.

"Well, I was talking with Larry DeLuca, and he had some interesting things to say."

"Such as?"

Les paused. Stendahl's gaze was steady, but Logan decided that yes, there was anxiety in his glare.

"Such as what he saw a certain night a long time ago. At the Hi-Di-Ho." Stendahl didn't respond, so Les kept going. "The night the bartender was killed."

"What night was that?"

"In January of '49. He didn't tell me the exact date."

Stendahl blanched for a moment, then recovered. His voice returned to normal: cold and hard. "That was a long time ago. Hard to remember so far back."

"Larry seems pretty clear on what he saw that night."

"And what was that?"

"He saw you knife the bartender."

Stendahl stared at Les for a long moment, then shook his head. "I don't think so."

"He did," Les insisted. Logan cringed at the desperation that had crept into the old man's voice. This was over.

Floyd Stendahl heard the same desperation and stood up. "No, he didn't. Larry DeLuca is long dead by now. I don't know what the hell you think you're doing..."

"He told me." Indignant, Les rose to face Stendahl. "He told me."

The face on Logan's screen smiled, a cold half-grin that didn't reach the eyes.

"No. You're playing a bullshit game with me." Stendahl's stare was brutal. "You've got nothing."

"I've got DeLuca's word!" Lester's voice quavered.

"Hah," spat Stendahl. "Is that all? I knew it. You don't have..." he paused for a beat. "Anything. You don't have anything." He turned and walked to the door. There was glare, then darkness, then glare again as Angela came inside.

One of the day drinkers stumbled outside. After thirty seconds, he spoke into Logan's ear. "They're gone."

30

I tried to convince myself that Lester Moore's failure to get a confession out of Floyd Stendahl wasn't a disaster. After all, it had been a Hail Mary play. Floyd wasn't the kind of guy who was likely to break down in front of an old man, suddenly deciding after six decades that his soul needed cleansing. And it could have ended much worse than Floyd storming out of the bar, me running after him to the car, and a hostile silence in the short drive back to his Gold Coast co-op.

The worse news came the next day, when I got a text from Logan saying he had been reassigned to some sort of special unit with a lot of overtime and no flexibility. Not only was he officially off the case, he was unofficially off it as well.

And I was stuck standing outside Bob Stendahl's office during the day and taking turns with Miguel and Henry walking around the Stendahls' yard at night. Every step around the yard reminded me of Bill, and not one step got me any closer to figuring out how to make things right, not for Bill, not for Angela's boss and Stu Mackenzie, not even for the poor guy in Uptown who'd had the bad luck to fall in love with the wrong heiress after World War II.

Charlie had asked each of us our assessment of the threat remaining to the client. His Russian sources, or at least his sources about the Russians—he was never forthcoming exactly which—reported that they weren't hearing much. I kept the fact that the FBI was monitoring our client to myself. Charlie stuck with the party line that Terrance Jones was a random robber, killed in action, and it was unlikely lightning would strike twice. Miguel and Henry agreed with the boss that the job now called for only two people and Charlie wanted me back in Florida. His stated reason was a new client, a female CEO who preferred a woman bodyguard, but I think he wanted me away from the Stendahls before I could cause trouble. Charlie was a little late on that count, but his reasoning wasn't wrong.

My communication with Angela and her aunt was limited to occasional texts.

"My CPD friends say Logan got transferred after Bob made a call," wrote Linda.

"What's Plan B? We can't let them get away with it." That one was Angela.

I typed "Sometimes the bad guys win," but thought the better of it and deleted the message before sending. Instead, I replied, "I don't know. Let me keep thinking."

Of course there was no Plan B. I had looked around the Stendahls' yard, hoping to find evidence linking Jones to Bob. Needless to say, I found nothing. With no evidence, no official police investigation and now not even unofficial help from Logan, I began to focus on how I would tell Angela and Linda that this was over.

My phone buzzed again.

"Any chance you can show me Chicago?" It was Mark. I realized how long it had been since we'd spent time together.

"I'd love to but now's not good." I hit Send before I could change my mind, so I added, "I miss you."

"Me, too."

I was considering a response when Mark texted again.

"I've got more information. Call me."

31

Mark is proof that sometimes you get lucky. Not just the normal definition of "getting lucky," although that, too. We had met in New Orleans where he led a walking tour I joined, and I offered him a drink as a tip. When I think of all the ways a pickup can go wrong—me dead in an alley, for instance—I realize that I won the lottery with Mark. He's smart, funny, good-looking in a rugged sort of way, a great lover, and not interested in a traditional relationship that would consist of us living together and me doing his laundry.

"How's New Orleans?" I asked by way of saying hello, stepping out onto the patio for a little privacy.

"Hot. Sticky. But only a couple more weeks before summer session is over and I get a break."

"Not so long ago you were thrilled to be teaching full-time."

"Yeah, and I still am. But breaks are good—especially when you know there's a full-time paycheck ahead."

"No doubt." I didn't want to bring up the case right away because I didn't want Mark to think I wasn't genuinely glad to talk with him. Still, my curiosity got the best of me, which it usually does. "You said you found something?"

"I have." He paused.

I gave him a couple of seconds to build the suspense before asking, "What is it?"

"Larry DeLuca died in Mexico in 1999."

"Oh." I felt as deflated as I had on Christmas morning when I was sixteen. I'd been sure I wasn't getting tickets to see the band Boston play at the Omaha Civic Auditorium, but it was still disappointing when I opened the package that had looked like a sweater to find only a sweater. "I had hoped maybe he'd still be living in a little town somewhere."

"Hanging out in front of the bus station and waiting for you to call?"

"I guess it was a ridiculous thought."

"Worth checking, however. But the good news is that I have something else to report."

"You never seem to give me bad news without having good news to follow, Mark. One of the things I like about you."

"And what are some of the others?" The smile in his voice made me smile, too.

"You'll have to wait on that. Right now I'm focused on…" As I was about to say "Chicago," I heard a click at the screen door. Suzi Stendahl stepped onto the patio. She offered me a tall glass of iced tea.

"Thought you might want something cold," she said.

"Thanks." I pulled the phone away from my ear and took the chilled glass. "I'm just checking in," I said to her. I didn't want to lie outright.

"Of course. I don't mean to interrupt you. Just thought you'd like some tea."

"Thanks," I repeated as she returned to the house. My gaze stayed on the door for a moment as I took a long sip, then I turned completely around to make sure I was alone again. "Sorry," I said to Mark. "What was the second thing?"

"I took a browse through the Cook County Jail's scheduling database, and found out they have an employee named Adam Marek who was working the night Terrance Jones was released."

It took me a minute to place the name. "Any relation to Alissa Marek, Stendahl Group's receptionist?"

"Brother."

"You're a miracle worker," I said.

"Not really. Before I started looking through the county records, I looked over the names of employees in Stendahl Group's corporate office. Glad they made it easy for me—the corporate office is relatively small. If it had been an employee from somewhere else in the company, from some other division, it would have required a lot more effort. Stendahl Group is huge."

"It is. And so is Cook County. What makes you think this isn't a coincidence?"

"Somebody from Stendahl Group called Adam Marek's cell the night Jones was arrested."

I stopped mid-sip. "That could just be Alissa calling her brother."

"Right, but unless the office was open late that night, unlikely. It was long after five. So I checked Bob Stendahl's cell phone records and found that he received a call from Cook County less than an hour after Jones got out." Mark paused, significantly. I played along, giving him a few dramatic seconds of silence.

"And?" I finally asked.

"Adam Marek really should use a stronger password for his online banking. He's lucky I'm an honest hacker, or I might have been tempted to take the six thousand dollars that he deposited a couple of days later." Mark laughed.

"That was a risky thing to do."

"Yeah, if I were going to do a favor like that for the Stendahls, I'd demand a lot more than six grand," said Mark.

"No, I mean hacking into a bank right now. I don't want you taking chances after your call the other day."

"Not to worry—I've changed things up a bit. I actually found a few steps I can take to make it nearly impossible for someone to track me."

"Be careful." I smiled at this, because Mark was usually the one to urge caution.

"Always."

My phone buzzed. Charlie.

"Mark, I've gotta go. Thank you."

"Can you repay me soon?" Mark dropped his voice half an octave and despite Charlie being on the other line, I felt a tingle between my legs.

"I hope so. I miss you, baby. Thanks again."

Charlie's voice jolted me back to reality as I switched calls. "I've talked with Bob Stendahl and they agree we don't need three men anymore."

Charlie referred to his employees in aggregate as men. Sometimes he said it out of habit, but mostly he did it when he wanted to piss me off.

"Good thing we don't have three men anymore." I regretted the words as soon as I said them, but I should have known Charlie was well past the memory of Bill's death.

"Ha ha. I need you back here. That lady CEO wants you to start Monday."

"Lady CEO?" I couldn't let Charlie get away with talking like it was 1985.

"Yeah," he said defensively. "Our new client."

"Your new client, you mean. Look, Charlie, I've been digging a little bit into Bill's murder."

"Murder? Bill was killed by a burglar. Line of duty. It wasn't murder."

"He was killed because he knew that Bob is up to something. I can prove that Bob arranged to get Terrance Jones released, and then got him to come to the house to make it look like a robbery in order to murder Bill." This was only a minor exaggeration.

"What the hell are you doing up there? I told you to drop it. The Stendahls are your clients, not the subjects of some crazy investigation you're playing around with. I've got a plane ticket in your name out of O'Hare tomorrow morning. You're coming home."

"I am not leaving Chicago until Bill's killer is punished. I owe him." I winced at how trite that sounded, but sometimes the truth is trite.

"You'll be on that plane at 8:57 a.m."

"Or what, Charlie?"

"You won't need to come back at all."

"That sounds like the better deal. I quit."

32

Linda Patterson's upstairs neighbor loved warm baths and chilled wine. If not, Linda might never have needed to dig out boxes that had been tucked in the back of a closet since she'd moved into her condo years earlier. But on Saturday afternoon she noticed a wet spot on the ceiling in her bathroom, near the wall. Maintenance confirmed that the source of the water was the tub above her, where her neighbor had dozed off with the bath overflowing the previous evening.

"Some of the water might have gone through the floor to the back closet," the maintenance man cautioned. "You should check."

Linda emptied the closet, moving clothes and boxes into her guest bedroom. The last two boxes had been there so long that she didn't even remember what was in them. Both initially seemed dry, and she opened them out of curiosity as much as concern.

She pulled out a couple of ironstone plates, white with a faded floral border. Her mother's good dishes, saved for guests and special occasions. Linda smiled and shook her head as the word "mother" came into her head. It was going to take a while to think of her mother as her aunt, and her mysterious aunt as her biological mother. She ran her fingers around the scalloped edges, deciding it was time to pull them out for her guests and her special occasions.

The second box contained a collection of Indiana glassware and carnival glass: platters, candy dishes, and a cream and sugar set. They were wrapped in tea towels, and a few towels were folded up as padding between the fragile pieces. Linda emptied the contents gently. She treasured the old tea towels as much as the dishes, spreading them open and refolding them. They were spotless. Linda remembered her mother—rather, her aunt—scrubbing out stains on laundry day.

Retrieving the last dish, she felt fabric that was much smoother than the cotton towels: a white silk scarf. She didn't remember her mother—aunt—having such a piece. She unfurled it and saw that it was more of an aviator scarf, longer than what a woman would have worn at the time the dishes had been packed away. She had never seen her father—uncle—in a scarf. Then she saw several rust-colored stains, and a monogram that confirmed it hadn't belonged to any of her relatives: FS.

33

I called Teresa during the twenty-minute cab ride from the Stendahls' home to O'Hare, which was the closest place to pick up a rental car on a Saturday evening.

"The guys said they'd try to let me know if anything happens," I said.

"Like Stendahl getting arrested?"

"Which Stendahl?" Sometimes my inner smart aleck just jumps out. "No, I don't think that's going to happen." I thought for a minute. "I guess I don't know what I think might happen. The Russians might come back. But Charlie seems to think that's unlikely, which is part of the reason he wanted me back in Miami."

"But the main reason was to keep you from investigating." Teresa could always cut to the chase.

"Exactly." I sighed as I swiped my credit card for the cabbie and handed him cash for the tip. Uncle Sam didn't need to know every bit of income the poor guy got. I stood outside the car rental building. "We're still good with our money, right?"

Teresa laughed. "Yes, we're fine. Tina, I've got that money in safe investments. We're not going to triple our money overnight, but we're not going to lose it, either."

"I know I shouldn't worry..."

"But you do. I get it—you're not used to having money. Don't worry. It's all under control."

Teresa's confidence made me feel better, but I still rented the cheapest car on the lot. And found a motel not too far from O'Hare that was under ninety dollars a night. Better safe than sorry.

Linda called while I was in the shower. When I returned the call, her voice was higher and louder than I'd heard her before.

"I found a scarf that has to be evidence Floyd Stendahl killed the man in Uptown," she began.

I stopped putting on eye liner. "What? A scarf?"

"Yes. It's got his initials on it, and what looks like old blood. It was in a box of family stuff. We need to give it to Logan."

"Have you spoken with him?"

"No, I've left him messages and texts. He's not responding. Can you come get us? I'm scared to be home with this thing."

"Who are you with?"

"Angela. Where are you? When can you get here?"

"I'm at a motel near O'Hare. Let me dress and I'll be on my way."

"Hurry."

"Keep trying Logan. Did you tell him why you wanted him to call you?"

"No. I haven't said anything about this except to Angela."

"Don't say anything to anyone else except Logan personally if he happens to call, and you should be fine. I'll meet you at your condo as soon as I can. I'm in a white Mitsubishi."

The trip turned out to be nearly an hour because of congested traffic on the Kennedy Expressway. I tried to see if I was being tailed, and the answer was, I *was* being followed, by about seven thousand other cars. It occurred to me that getting a car with an underpowered four-cylinder engine may have been a mistake, since I wouldn't have a chance if I needed to outrun or follow anybody in a vehicle more powerful than a bicycle. But on the Kennedy, inching along, it didn't matter.

The Dan Ryan Expressway moved better, but the traffic was still heavy enough that I couldn't notice any particular car; if someone was following me, I couldn't tell. When I exited at 18th Street, however, a silver Dodge Charger exited, too. The address Linda had texted me was north of 18th on State Street so I turned south instead, away from her condo, noting the Chicago Police Department station on the corner. The Charger kept going straight on 18th. I drove a block until I could make a U-turn and head north to Linda's. I pulled into a space on the street in front of her building, right behind another car that was already parked. Linda and Angela must have been waiting in the lobby because they ran outside when they saw me pull up.

Before I could completely stop, I felt a bump from behind and heard metal scraping against metal. I looked in the rearview mirror and saw a silver car behind me. The driver was a blond man who looked familiar, but I didn't know why. I jammed on the brakes which accomplished nothing; I was pushed into the parked car ahead. A woman screamed. I jumped out of the Mitsubishi and saw another man, a bag in his hand, dive into the Charger as it backed up and drove away, nearly hitting me in the process.

"He's got the scarf!" shouted Linda. She and Angela each grabbed a door and leapt into my car, Linda in the front and Angela in the back. I looked at the grill of the rental, and while it was damaged, it looked drivable. I returned to the driver's seat and started the engine.

"Hurry! He's heading north!" Angela directed from the back. I floored it, although it took a moment to get up to fifty miles per hour. The proximity to the police station made me think we'd see cops, but we didn't. Traffic on State Street was light and I made it the few blocks to Roosevelt in no time, with two cars between us and the Charger. The blond turned east onto Roosevelt, which looked like a parking lot. I snaked around one car and was blocked by a second. My tiny white rental didn't have much pickup, but at least it was easy to maneuver in heavy traffic.

"He's signaling to turn left onto Michigan," called Angela.

The light turned green after an eternity and I forced my way into the left lane so I would be behind him, enduring horns and a blistering description of my mother in the process.

"No, he's going straight," Angela yelled.

More horns, but I made it out of the turn lane so we could follow him eastbound toward the Lake.

"I can't believe he's got the scarf. How could he know to get it?" Linda asked herself more than Angela or me. "How?"

"Was he following you?" Angela asked. I couldn't tell whether she was asking or accusing.

There were now three cars between us and the Charger. Amazingly, I was able to speed around one of them at an intersection. "Yes, he was. But how would he know to grab the scarf?"

"Is your phone tapped?" Angela asked.

I decided she was simply asking, not accusing. But she wouldn't have needed to beat me up at that point anyway; I recognized how stupid I'd been.

"Dammit, I should have figured they were. Stendahl's company certainly has the technology to do that themselves, don't they?"

"Absolutely," Angela confirmed. "Especially a cell phone."

"Shit. I'm sorry." Neither woman had a chance to reply as I saw the Charger turn right onto Lake Shore Drive and I cut across two lanes of traffic to follow him. "Where do you think he's going?" I asked.

"I have no idea," said Linda.

"No, I mean is there a road that he's likely to get on from here?"

"Oh, yes, probably I-55 and then either stay on the Stephenson Expressway or go south on the Ryan. Just stay to the right."

I maneuvered around traffic so we were right behind the Charger. He hung in the middle of Lake Shore Drive as we passed Soldier Field and the exit for the McCormick Place convention center.

"Do we want him to stay on Lake Shore? Would it be easier to follow him that way?" I asked as I cut him off to the right, so that we were between him and the upcoming I-55 exit. Before anyone answered, he floored it, cut in front of me, and sailed onto the ramp toward the interstate. I followed, but kept losing ground against the superior engine of the Charger.

I-55 begins at Lake Shore Drive and immediately becomes a complex road of merging and splitting traffic as it curves around the monstrous McCormick Place. I was nearly side-swiped by traffic entering the interstate from the convention center, and before recovering heard Angela yell, "he's getting off on the Ryan."

The silver Charger was in the lane marked for Indiana and points south. He'd had to slow down for the merging traffic, too, which let me speed up to his tail. He approached the cloverleaf, me close behind. Then, just before the road split, he bounded back into westbound traffic, causing a delivery van behind him to slow down and honk. That van, followed by another car, kept me from being able to jerk back onto I-55. Linda shouted "no!" from the backseat as we curved onto the Dan Ryan Expressway, southbound, and helpless.

34

We got off the Ryan by the White Sox stadium, crossed over on 37th Street, and headed back north toward Linda's. Her cell rang.

"Logan," she announced before answering.

"A little late," Angela grumbled. I thought the same thing.

Linda ignored her. "Hi, James." Her voice sounded like she was talking with a casual friend who was inviting her to a movie. She said "uh-huh" twice, with a long break in between. Then, "James, there *is* evidence. It's a scarf with Floyd Stendahl's monogram, and what looks like a blood stain." She was quiet. "No. I don't have it anymore. This guy grabbed it and we tried to catch up but we lost him." More quiet. "But I can describe what I saw. Wouldn't that be enough to at least question him?" I glanced over to the passenger seat. Linda was shaking her head, her lips tightened. "No, I guess not. Okay, James, thanks for letting me know."

"What?" Angela was leaning through the space between the front seats, turned toward her aunt.

"He said there's nothing to be done. Someone's been making calls. Even if we still had the scarf, he said he didn't think it would matter, and without it, well..."

"You mean CPD's fixed the case?" Now Angela sounded accusatory, although not toward Linda, who simply nodded sadly.

"Yes. It's over."

"It can't be! That man killed somebody, and my grandfather—your father—took the fall for it. And then they killed Krista, and Stu..." Angela started to cry.

Linda reached back with her arm around the younger woman and there were two sets of sobs.

"Assholes," I said, because I couldn't think of anything better to say. "When we get back to your place we can come up with a plan."

"No," sniffled Linda. "I don't want to go home. What if they're still watching us?"

"I doubt they are anymore," I said before realizing that being sensible wasn't very sympathetic. I recovered with "Let's go to my hotel. At least we'll be in public."

My phone rang before we reached the Jane Byrne Circle, where the Eisenhower Expressway connects with the Dan Ryan and the Kennedy. Despite it being late on a Saturday night, traffic was still moving slowly. I sighed when I saw the caller ID, popped my Bluetooth earpiece in and answered.

"Hello, Charlie."

"Where are you?"

"What? No 'how's everything?'"

"I don't have time for bullshit, Tina. Where are you?"

"I'm in heavy traffic in Chicago." I paused. "Since you've got me on the phone I should tell you: physical evidence exists of your client's murder of a man in the 1940's."

"I'm a lot more interested in the fact that my Russian source said they're back on the hunt for our clients."

"*Your* clients, Charlie. They're not mine anymore." But I felt a twinge of concern for Suzi.

"So you don't care about Suzi Stendahl?"

I knew Charlie would play that card. I couldn't even hate him for it; it would be like hating a dog for pulling food off the counter. It was just his nature.

"Aren't Miguel and Henry with them?"

"Yes, but I need a third man."

"You had a third man, Charlie. And your client had him killed."

"Tina, you know what I mean." He dropped his voice, which he often did when he tried to sound convincing. "We need you."

"Charlie, Miguel and Henry are perfectly capable of handling this."

"Miguel said when he told the Stendahls about the situation, Suzi asked for you."

This was plausible, but it wasn't clear to me whether it was true.

"What's happening with the Russians?" I asked.

He paused. Angela and Linda were both staring at me.

"Charlie, you need to level with me for a change. Do you want me back or not?"

"You're acting like I've got a choice, Tina." Charlie's voice rose from strain. "The Russians...there's a new man that arrived earlier today. My source...well, he said this guy doesn't miss."

That sounded more like the truth.

"Look, I've got people in the car I need to drop off. I'll do that and be at the Stendahls' in an hour."

"Thanks, Tina. I owe you."

There was no point in responding, so I punched the off button on the Bluetooth and told my passengers about the change of plans.

35

Floyd Stendahl

Floyd Stendahl had several lady friends—his lovelies, he called them—and spent Saturday evening entertaining one of them at Gene & Georgetti on Franklin. Ever the gentleman, he had his driver drop the lady at her Streeterville condo before going home to his own Sullivanesque style brick and terra cotta co-op in the Gold Coast. His unit was positioned to give him a full view of Lake Michigan and a view of the city as well.

Floyd nodded to the smiling uniformed man who held the door for him. The co-op's lobby was an aging beauty. A giant bouquet of mums, hyacinths, and pink lilies on a round wooden table under a chandelier brightened the room, which was otherwise dominated by dark wood paneling.

"Good evening, Mr. Stendahl."

"Good evening, Juan."

"A friend stopped by to see you earlier."

"Who?" Except for his lovelies and a couple of guys from the Standard Club, none of whom was likely to drop by unannounced, Floyd Stendahl didn't have any friends.

"Your Russian friend. Tim was on duty when he came by. The man told Tim and Tim told me to say your Russian friend stopped in, and you'd know who I was talking about." Floyd froze. Juan, experienced in reading the moods of his employers, immediately dropped his smile. "Are you okay, Mr. Stendahl?"

Floyd willed himself to say, "Yes, Juan. I'm fine." He paused. "When did he stop by?"

"Tim said around six-thirty. Definitely before seven, 'cause that's when I came on."

"Juan, that man was not a friend. He is threatening me."

"Should I call the police, Mr. Stendahl?" Juan's face firmed up with the challenge.

"No. No cops. I've got private security from the company. I'll call them in."

"Are you sure? You want me to come upstairs with you? Check things out?"

"No. I'll be fine." But Floyd's voice wasn't confident.

"It's no trouble, Mr. Stendahl. Better safe than sorry, right?"

"Yes, I guess I would appreciate it. Thanks, Juan." The two men walked through glass doors to the elevator, Juan leading the way and wondering what Mr. Stendahl had gotten himself into.

36

Traffic was crawling on the Kennedy, so we'd not made it as far as North Avenue when my cell buzzed again. Henry.

"Yeah, Henry. I'm on my way."

"We need you to go to Floyd Stendahl's place instead. Now. A Russian stopped over to see him earlier."

"When? Is he okay?"

"He's fine. The guy stopped by while Stendahl was out at dinner. But he's scared shitless. I'm staying with Bob and Suzi, and Miguel is on his way into town. Stendahl lives a little north of the Magnificent Mile. Do you have his address?"

"Text me. I'm not very far from downtown. It shouldn't take me long to get there." Russians or not, the opportunity to see Floyd Stendahl was not to be missed. "I'll let you know when I arrive." I wasn't sure what to do about my passengers, but Henry didn't need to know about them.

"Good. And be careful."

I hung up. "Plan C, ladies," I said. "I need to go to Floyd Stendahl's and don't have time to take you to the motel."

"Floyd Stendahl's?" Linda and Angela spoke at the same time.

"Yup. He's got some very scary people after him."

"Seems like justice," said Angela.

"I thought you'd quit working for them," Linda said.

"I thought I did, too. But apparently the Russians are back, or at least one of them, and it's an all-hands sort of night. Plus it's a chance to talk with the old man."

"Yes, I want to talk with him." Angela's voice was firm.

"No, you won't be talking with him. It's a dangerous situation. These are the same people who kidnapped Suzi Stendahl and me. They're not to be messed with. I think it would be best if I dropped you at a Starbucks."

"No," said both women.

"I don't think you understand. The guy after Stendahl is a killer."

"Then we should call Logan," said Linda.

"That's a good idea. Why don't you call him?" I doubted she would get through, but it was worth trying.

Linda was dialing before I finished. "This is Linda Patterson. Again. Please call me."

"What's going on with him?" I cursed at a car that slowed through an intersection so I missed the light.

"I don't know what the problem is," she said.

I cursed again as we turned south onto LaSalle and nearly rear-ended an Uber that was stopped on the street.

"You okay?" asked Angela.

"Yeah, it's just these idiots you let drive in this city."

"They're better in Miami?"

"Fair point. But right now I'm dealing with Chicago idiots, not Miami idiots." I sighed. "Mostly I'm just stressed about what's happening with Floyd. I can't believe I'm going to try to help him when what he needs is to be locked up."

"For four murders," Angela said.

"And making my dad leave my mom," said Linda. Angela patted her shoulder, and Linda reached up to grip her niece's hand.

"Assholes," was all I could say.

Logan knew exactly why he'd been detailed to a series of gang murders on the West Side, and it wasn't because CPD brass cared much about the fate of five young black men with the bad fortune of being born in the impoverished North Lawndale neighborhood. He'd put in thirty-six hours in three days, and told his wife Ramona that Monday he was calling his union rep to complain. At his age, the overtime pay wasn't worth it. Ramona was nice enough not to remind him how long she'd been telling him the same thing.

So when he finally got home Saturday night he turned off his phone and turned on the television. Ramona had cooked peppers and sausage, one of his favorites, and had filled the refrigerator with beer. Together they watched the White Sox lose to the Royals, and Logan began to think that retirement sounded pretty sweet.

Tom Donnelly was waiting in the lobby of his uncle's building when we arrived. He smiled with relief as I walked in, his expression turning to confusion when he saw Angela and Linda trailing me.

"Thanks for coming. My uncle's upstairs, and I don't think I've ever seen him scared like this." He shook my hand awkwardly, looking like he was trying to decide whether a hug would be appropriate. He looked beyond me. "Who are these ladies?"

"Angela Frank and Linda Patterson." There wasn't a quick explanation for why they were with me, so I attempted none.

"Okay." Tom drew out the syllables.

"It's a long story, but they're going to stay in the lobby while I go upstairs and wait with Mr. Stendahl until Miguel gets here."

Tom shrugged and motioned to the doorman who was standing at his station on full alert. "Juan will watch them."

"We don't need to be watched," protested Linda. Then, to me, more quietly, "I thought we were going upstairs."

"Until I know what's happening, I think that's a bad idea."

"We want to talk with Floyd," Angela said firmly. "That's why we're here."

"About what?" Tom asked.

"About what happened in 1949," I said to Tom. He raised his eyebrows to me and I nodded. "They found evidence."

"God." Tom's face went flat, and I couldn't tell if he was afraid or relieved.

"So you know why we need to talk with him." Linda wasn't asking.

Tom shook his head slowly, but in amazement, not denial. "After all this time," he said, nearly under his breath.

Angela and Linda moved to the glass doors that led to the elevator vestibule. I realized I wasn't going to keep them out, and rationalized that maybe they were safer upstairs, anyway. "He's up there alone, Floyd is?"

Tom nodded.

I turned to the doorman. "Is there another way into the building? A loading dock or something?"

"Yes, in the back, but it takes a key to get in."

Unless somebody propped the door open for convenience, I thought. "Is anyone moving in or out today?"

The doorman shook his head. "Our owners let me know if they need anything taken through there." The way he said "owners" clearly communicated his disdain at my lack of understanding how a building as important as his worked. I let that go, because it was good news that a stranger was unlikely to be let in under the pretense of being a mover or making a delivery.

"Sounds like you run a tight ship," was my apology.

"Yes, ma'am. This isn't a condo or a rental building. It's a co-op. Everybody's been here a long time and looks out for each other," was his acceptance.

"Juan, can you please let us upstairs?" Tom asked the man. "You've got my cell number; if the Russian shows up, please call me."

Juan looked toward Angela and Linda. Tom nodded his approval. Juan's face expressed doubt as to the wisdom of letting these two women, clearly adversaries of his employer, upstairs, but he followed Tom's instruction and buzzed us through the glass doors.

No one spoke in the elevator. I was considering how this could play out, and everyone else was lost in their own thoughts as we rose to the ninth floor. Tom courteously let the ladies off first, directing us down a hallway carpeted in gray and lavender. The walls were ivory, with curved molding softening the line of the ceiling. The effect let you know you were among people with money and taste.

"At the end of the hall on the left," said Tom.

"Let me go first," I said quietly to Tom as we approached, pulling my gun from my shoulder bag. No point in being overconfident in Juan's opinion of the building's security. I listened at the door. There was some talking, then a crack. I grabbed the knob just as the noise inside turned into a dull roar. A crowd. Baseball on television. I smiled, breathed, put the gun back in the bag, and knocked.

"Mr. Stendahl? It's Tina Johnson and Tom. Henry asked me to stop by."

The door opened a minute later. Floyd Stendahl wore a dark blue suit without a tie. Compared to his normal attire at the office, this was casual.

"Took you long enough." The four of us entered. "Who are these two?"

"Friends of mine," I said. His tone annoyed me. "I don't work for you anymore, and I was with them when Henry called and said it was urgent."

"You normally bring friends to work?"

"As I said, I don't work for you anymore. I'm here because Henry asked, and because I believe that business dealings gone wrong shouldn't be resolved by violence, no matter how illegal the business was."

Floyd glared at Tom. "What did you tell her?"

"This isn't about Tom. It's actually about Krista Jordan and Stuart Mackenzie and Bill Bauer and a bartender in 1949. And Terrance Jones, for that matter."

Floyd's eyes widened for a second, then narrowed. He took a step back and grabbed the back of an overstuffed chair for support, but said nothing.

"And my father, Larry DeLuca," said Linda.

Tom tilted his head. "Who are those people, Krista and what did you say, Stuart? And what does Floyd have to do with Bill?"

"Krista Jordan was my boss, and Stu Mackenzie was a friend." Angela took a half step toward Floyd as she spoke.

I stepped in front of Angela, to keep her from moving closer. The last thing you need in an emotionally volatile situation is to have people in arm's reach of each other. Besides, I had my own score to settle. "You know Bill Bauer," I said to Floyd. "He worked with me. He died in a set-up, trying to protect Bob and Suzi." I didn't know whether Floyd ever knew any of our names, or whether he cared.

"And Larry DeLuca was my grandfather." Angela glared at Floyd from behind me. To Tom she said, "Your uncle and your cousin had Krista and Stu and Bill killed, and framed my grandfather for a murder so he had to leave my grandmother."

"And me," added Linda, her voice soft. "He had to leave me."

Angela stepped around me to her aunt's side, putting her arm around Linda.

"Larry DeLuca was a thug," snarled Floyd. "You were better off without him."

"He and my mother loved each other," said Linda. "They were going to marry."

Floyd laughed. He had let go of the couch and recovered his dominance. "No. Wasn't going to happen. Not even a thug's family would accept him marrying a ni—" Floyd looked at Linda. *It's my choice not to say the word,* his cold smile seemed to say. *It's up to me, not you.*

Angela jumped in before Linda could speak. "How did you know?"

"We had a black maid, Edna, from Bronzeville, and one day I was with her walking down Bryn Mawr. Edna saw a girl she recognized from her neighborhood, and tried to speak with the girl. The girl acted like she didn't know Edna, said she was working at the Edgewater and didn't know anything about Bronzeville or Edna. That made Edna mad, and she told me that this girl was passing as white. I'd never heard of that before. I'd see the girl from time to time and remembered what Edna had said. That girl was with DeLuca in the bar." Floyd corrected himself with a sneer. "Maybe."

Nobody spoke. All eyes were glued on the old man, who seemed to be enjoying himself.

He continued. "So for a moment, let's just assume that the thug and his *girlfriend* saw something happen in the bar." Floyd uttered *girlfriend* with so much insulting innuendo that I nearly hit him. Linda and Angela stood frozen, waiting for the rest of the story. "They might have thought they could tell the police what they might have seen. But that's not how it works, is it? I knew their secret. And if I had told DeLuca's family, there was no way they would have allowed the marriage. They weren't going to be together no matter what, and Larry was smart enough to understand that. He was also smart enough to understand he'd be fingered for the bartender. And if he hadn't been smart enough, perhaps I helped make it clear: the way he could protect his woman's secret was by disappearing. A criminal who'd done time for robbing the same bar? And who then took off? That was all the cops needed to stop worrying about some dead bartender in Uptown."

Tom was pale, and stared at the floor. Angela remained silent, holding onto her aunt. Linda squared her shoulders. She had heard enough.

"There's evidence," she said. "I found the scarf. Your scarf. The one you were wearing that night. It has blood stains on it."

Floyd shook his head in disgust. "Evidence, you say? A scarf? Perhaps one that I might have realized was missing the next morning? One that I might have thought they had kept. But it didn't matter, because I would have had as much on her as she had on me. I mean, hypothetically, of course. It was what they call a Mexican stand-off. An ironic phrase, isn't it?" He snorted at his own wit. "She'd have lost her job if I'd told her secret, and she certainly knew that I could talk my way around the cops better than some ni—" he glanced at Linda and Angela again "—than some knocked up hotel maid."

Angela slapped him.

Floyd allowed his face a slight turn with the impact, then slowly recovered and looked closely at her. "And you, young woman, you were with that old man who tried to shake me down." He considered this for a moment, then returned to the matter at hand. "You say you have a scarf? Why don't you show it to me?"

We were silent.

"I thought so," he said. "There's no goddamned scarf." Then he formed his lips into a sneer. "Or maybe there used to be a scarf, but it was recently destroyed." Linda blanched, which made Floyd laugh coldly. "So don't tell me about some damned scarf." He turned to Tom. "What the hell were you thinking letting these people come up here?"

Tom said nothing. His demeanor turned from middle aged man to a child waiting to be punished.

We all started slightly from the knock at the door.

"Mr. Stendahl, it's Adam. Everything okay?"

Floyd crossed to the door and opened it. In walked the male version of Alissa Marek, Stendahl Group's receptionist. The driver of the silver Charger.

"Adam Marek?" I asked.

"Yes," he said, before he could decide not to.

"You still working at Cook County?"

Marek blinked. This time he recovered himself before speaking.

"You're the one who let Terrance Jones get bailed out, right?" I asked. "It's hard to keep all that paperwork straight."

Marek moved toward me but Floyd held up his hand.

"You're the one who stole the scarf! What did you do with it?" Linda stepped toward the smirking blond man but Angela pulled her back.

"That's enough. The three of you get out. Get the hell out." Floyd was herding us toward the door. "Tom, you stay here. I've got some things I want to say to you."

39

Linda, Angela, and I stood in the wide doorway of the apartment building next door to the co-op, waiting for Miguel, who was still stuck in traffic. Floyd had called Juan and told him to make us leave the lobby, which Juan seemed happy to do.

Floyd's disclosures were the kind that begged a long family debrief, and I sensed that Linda and Angela wanted to do so.

"Go get some coffee or a drink or something," I urged them.

"Not now," said Linda firmly. "We can discuss this after everything is over."

"It would be better if you left. I don't want you in the middle of whatever mess the Russians have in mind."

"We're not leaving you to deal with this by yourself," Angela said.

Before I could make another attempt, Linda held her hand up. "It's decided," she said. "We're not leaving you alone."

"I appreciate the extra eyes," I relented. "But that's all. Help me look out for this guy, and that's it. When he shows up, please let me handle it."

The street was busy, so it didn't hurt to have a couple of extra spotters. The crowd was made up of twenty-somethings, out to explore on a Saturday night, and older people on their way home after theater or dinner. With those two demographics, the three of us blended in. I kept my back to Stendahl's co-op, with Angela and Linda reporting any activity at the door. Depending on who "the Russian" was, he might recognize me, but he wouldn't know them.

Angela announced quietly that two older women were walking into the co-op. About two minutes later, she said, "Now there's an elderly lady going in alone. No, there's a man right behind her. Tina, look."

I turned in time to see a short, silver-haired woman with a look of panic on her face. Immediately behind her, one hand on her shoulder and another touching her back, was a man wearing a dark windbreaker. His face was turned from mine, and his hair was dark. The streetlight's glare made it difficult to tell the exact shade. He took his hand—pale skin tone—from her shoulder long enough to yank open the door, pushing her in.

"Stay here," I ordered, with little hope of being obeyed. I moved closer, where I could look through the front window of the co-op. Juan's face was ashen. The woman and man were already through the glass doors to the elevator. They turned sideways and I saw a gun in the man's hand, pressed against the woman's back.

"What's going on?" asked Angela. She had moved between where I was and where her aunt remained, twenty feet away. She stepped closer so she could hear me.

"That has to be the guy. He used that old woman to push himself in."

"Is she okay?"

"I don't know. They're just getting into the elevator. Tell Linda to call Logan, and you call 911."

Angela ran to her aunt and they both pulled out their phones. I pushed through the front door of the co-op. Juan was shaking.

"That man with Mrs. Cohn, was he...the one?" Juan asked.

"Yes, I think it's the guy who was here earlier. Call 911 and let me get back upstairs to Stendahl's." Multiple emergency calls might speed up response, I thought.

He picked up the phone as the buzzer signaled I could enter the elevator vestibule. I dialed Tom's cell number but it went to voicemail. Next to the bank of elevators was a door marked "Stair." Pulling my gun from my bag, I slowly opened the door. No sound, no response. I stepped into a cement stairwell and started up.

As I reached the fourth floor, I took a half-second break to look around. Above me, somewhere, I heard a door open and fast-moving footsteps. Returning to my climb, I moved quickly while trying to keep an eye upward.

That is easier said than done, and I heard the shot before I saw the gun, pointed down over the stair rail three or four flights above me. It went wild, and I couldn't tell how far below me it hit. I jumped back and forth as I ran up the stairs in an effort to be a serpentine target, but mostly stayed to the inside, making me harder to reach from above.

"Cops are on their way," I called, hoping that the echo from the hard walls would disorient the shooter, at least a little. I didn't want to return fire until I could see who I was shooting at.

The response was another bullet. This one hit the wall behind me. I shrugged my bag off my shoulder to the floor, and ran to the next landing. There, I backed into the corner, where the shooter would have a tougher angle. A small metal ant trap lay on the floor. I threw it down the stairs to direct his attention away from me. Two more shots.

In the movies they always count the bullets, but in real life it doesn't work that way: I didn't know what kind of weapon I was up against, and had no idea how many bullets had been fired before he started. Maybe he had a second weapon. Not knowing his capabilities, I would have to stay clear of him until I could find a good shot, or until help arrived.

The gun barrel over the railing now wasn't more than two flights above me. I aimed my weapon toward the landing ahead of me and waited.

40

Logan's wife sighed deeply when he turned his phone back on after the game ended, but it's hard to change a career of habits in one evening. He scrolled through a half-dozen texts, including several from his old coworker, Linda Patterson. He was considering how to reply when the phone rang. It was the number from which Linda had been texting him, so he answered.

"Logan."

"James, it's Linda. We're at Lake Shore and Goethe. Floyd Stendahl's building. There's a man with a gun who's threatened him and is upstairs."

"Did you call 911?"

"Angela's calling now."

"What are you doing there?"

"We were with Tina and she got called. Some Russian guy—she thought that maybe it was one of the guys who kidnapped her."

"She texted me that she'd quit."

"She did quit, but they called her anyway. We were in the car with her."

Logan switched her to Bluetooth and pulled on a pair of slacks. His wife looked resigned.

"Baby, I'm sorry," said Logan. "If it weren't Linda Patterson—you remember her, right?"

"What?" asked Linda.

"No, not you—I'm talking with Ramona."

"What should I do?" Linda was trying not to wail, with limited success.

"Text me the address and stay outside. It'll take me twenty minutes, but I'll be there."

41

The shooter stood in the opposite corner of the landing above me, where neither of us could see the other's face, but where I could see the black tip of his gun barrel, poking out from the stairs. We were both waiting. For what, I wasn't sure. For the cops to show up? For one of us to miscalculate? Although I didn't know the man with the gun, I assumed he had more experience in these situations than I did since the number of previous gun fights I'd had in a stairwell was exactly zero. That made waiting prudent, but not without its own risks. The Russian, or whoever he was, had to expect the cops to be on their way, which meant he was probably motivated to make something happen so he could get out. After a minute that seemed like an hour, I decided to go first.

"Who the hell are you?" I yelled up. I wasn't expecting an answer, but hoped I could provoke him to do…something.

The barrel lengthened, inching toward me. The only question was which of us would be in the other's sight first. There was no noise in the stairwell, and I trusted that the elderly population of the building was unlikely to be running up or down to the laundry room at ten o'clock on a Saturday night.

"Who the hell are you?" I asked again, my gun still raised. I stepped forward so I could look up and see him. He was white with a face that had hardened too young. His eyes locked on mine, and we both fired. I immediately ducked back, hoping to change the angle between us, nearly deafened by the sound ricocheting against the concrete walls. The noise was disorienting and it took a moment to realize that I was still standing. Then silence, and I wondered whether the cracks from the bullets had deafened me until I heard a grunt from the landing above. Maybe I had hit him, but he was still alive.

Raising my weapon, I retreated to my earlier position in the corner of the landing, ready to fire again. He moaned. Had I shot him, or was he trying to draw me out? The only way to know was to get closer. I pressed against the wall and took a step up, and paused. Another moan. I took the next step, and the next. Halfway up the flight, I could see him.

The man had sunk to the floor of the landing, sitting feet-out, back against the gray wall. His head drooped on his chest and his arms were at his sides. His black pistol rested loosely in his right hand, and I didn't see any blood. I fired again, aiming above him. At the blast, his head jerked to attention and his eyes opened. Clear, alert. The corner of his mouth turned up in a cold smile, which chilled me to the bone. By coming forward, I had fallen into his trap. Despite the fact I had my 9 mm Luger trained on him, I felt like his prey. Running away was not possible; he would easily be able to pick me off before I could get out of his line of fire.

But I had the half-second advantage of having my weapon ready to fire, versus him still holding his pistol at his side. And I was standing, more easily mobile than he was. The man's stare remained confident, arrogant, but his leer disappeared. Perhaps this wasn't playing out exactly as he had hoped.

"I don't want to kill you," I said. We were eye-level; him seated, and me a few steps below the landing.

"I don't want to be killed." He spoke with a Russian accent, and his smile returned for a moment. "But you are a pain in my ass. Which is why I am going to kill you."

His right hand moved quickly and I fired into his chest, then leapt down to the landing below to get out of his view. I could hear my own heavy breathing, but nothing else.

Still holding the Luger in front of me, I walked back up the flight one step at a time, hugging the inside of the stairway; from where he was seated the angle would be nearly impossible for him to shoot me. I was sure I had hit him, but darted my head around the railing to make sure.

I saw the Russian still sitting against the wall. His head sagged, chin on his sternum, dark blood staining his white shirt, spreading under his unzipped jacket. His right arm had fallen into his lap, still holding the pistol.

I repositioned my Luger for another shot, attention focused on his gun, taking the last stairs very slowly. Once on the landing, I moved closer, keeping my eyes and weapon trained on him. His chest was still: he wasn't breathing. I stared at his body and counted to thirty. No movement. I took another step toward him. No movement.

I waited another thirty seconds before approaching him further. I could smell powder burns along with the slightly metallic scent of blood as I reached down to grab his weapon. Tucking my Luger in my back waistband, I emptied the magazine of his pistol and slid the action to pop out the round that was inside. I tucked his weapon in my waistband as well, next to the Luger.

I bent over and touched the side of his neck. Nothing. I pressed a little harder. Nothing.

Without thinking, I backed away until I was against a wall, as far away from the body as I could be without leaving the landing. My palms were pressed against the rough cement, but I knew the clammy feeling in my hands was not from the concrete.

I had never killed anyone before. I felt angry that he put me in a position where I had no choice. Then I remembered why I was there, and I swore at him under my breath as I ran up the stairs to see what destruction he had wrought on the ninth floor.

In case the Russian hadn't been alone, I was cautious opening the door into the hallway. It was empty, except for Adam Marek's body just outside Floyd Stendahl's door. A dark stain covered the gray and lavender carpeting next to him. The co-op's door had been forced open and inside I saw Stendahl lying on the floor, blood pooling around him. Sirens wailed, close enough that I hoped they were heading for us and not somebody else's tragedy.

"Tina?" The voice was Tom's, and was weak. It came from the far side of the main room.

I turned to see Tom Donnelly on the ground, pulling himself around a gray couch that had looked better before bullets pierced its upholstery.

"Tom, are you okay?"

"Yes. I mean no, I was shot, but I'm alive. What about Floyd? And Adam?"

Tom's view of his uncle had been blocked by the couch.

"He's been shot, and it looks bad. Adam is dead."

"Uncle Floyd?" Tom called out. Tom had been hit in one leg and the other arm. He was bleeding, but not as much as the older man sprawled on the floor.

I didn't get a chance to respond before several voices began yelling "CPD."

42

Much to the doorman's distress, James Logan turned the co-op's lobby into a temporary office, appropriating a black leather couch and dark wooden coffee table. The table held his notebook, his phone, and a half-finished cup of coffee. The couch held his large frame, and the last person to leave the scene after everyone else had packed up. She was leaning forward and looked exhausted. Logan didn't blame her.

"I don't think you need to worry about Vasily Popov," he said to Tina. "Tom Donnelly identified him as the man who shot him and his uncle. He didn't see who shot Adam Marek, but since the doorman didn't see anyone beside him go upstairs, we're comfortable that the ballistics will match his weapon." Tina didn't say anything. Logan shifted on the leather to look more directly at her. "Have you ever killed anyone before?"

She shook her head. "No."

"This was as righteous as they come, but that doesn't make it easy."

"Have you?" She looked at him and sounded younger than her face appeared.

"Yes. It was years ago, but I still think about it. You need to get past it, but not get used to it. Does that make sense?"

"It does." Tina smiled slowly, then more broadly, and nodded. "I guess it does."

They sat without speaking and Logan sipped his coffee.

"The pieces seem to fit together," he said. "At least, the pieces I'm concerned about. It's up to the Feds whether they want to investigate Stendahl Group for selling illegal technology. But in terms of state crime, we've got a gangster who killed three people, including your partner, and was killed himself during the commission of that felony. We've got another gangster who killed two people, shot a third, and died in the act of attempted homicide of a fourth person, you. And whether Floyd Stendahl killed a man in 1949 is now between his soul and his God."

"But where does that leave Bob Stendahl? He was behind killing Bill and Krista and Stu. And for that matter, I think he set up Terrance Jones."

"Says who? There's no evidence of any of that. I understand your theory, and I might even agree with it, but his tracks are completely covered. Whether that's luck or skill I don't know, and it doesn't matter. We even interviewed the receptionist—Alissa, her name is, right?—and she hasn't said anything that makes us think she was involved. Truly, I think she didn't know about it. She said Bob had met Adam a year or so ago when he came up to the office to see her, but she didn't seem to know that they'd been in contact since."

Tina shook her head. "So you're just going to take her word for it? Is that what you do with other witnesses? Or only if they might implicate billionaires?"

Logan stared at her and shrugged. "Look, I'm just telling you the way it is. I don't like it any more than you do, but I know how things work. The investigation is closed."

43

Logan may have said it was closed, but I couldn't accept that. Bob Stendahl was responsible for four deaths, including one of my best friends. Maybe I couldn't connect him to anything now, but I wasn't ready to pack up and let him go.

"I think I'm moving to Chicago," I told Teresa when I checked in with her the next day.

"Chicago? Really? You like winter that much?" Teresa had lived in the South her entire life.

"What can I say? I'm a Midwesterner at heart. Summer in Miami is too hot, and I like the change of seasons."

"I've been to Chicago a few times, for work. It's not a bad city." She paused. "I have some news, too."

"What?"

"Gave my notice at the bank."

"No way!" I was glad I was sitting down, because this was most unexpected. "Congratulations! What made you finally decide to take the leap?"

"Last time we talked I felt jealous of you. You were up in Chicago having adventures, and I was stuck here. Then I realized how dumb that was—there's nothing holding me here at all. Other than getting the house painted." She laughed. "And they're coming tomorrow. A friend of a friend is a realtor, and once the painters are done I'm having her come over to look. I want to list it in early August."

"That is really big news," I said. "Where are you planning to go? Miami?" I hoped she'd say no to that, since I wouldn't be there anymore, but if you've lived in the South your whole life, the thought of a Chicago winter might be too much.

"Well, I had been. But if you're not there it won't be as much fun. Maybe I'll just travel around a while. Come up to Chicago, even, and see if I like it. I want to take a page from your book, and go on an adventure."

"As long as I'm in Chicago, you've always got a place to stay. At least, after I find a place, myself."

I was smiling at Teresa's decision as I called Mark. I figured he would be supportive of my decision to stay in Chicago, because he always was supportive, but his response surprised me as much as Teresa's.

"My daughter and her husband moved from Ohio to Indianapolis, and she's having a baby this winter. I hadn't said anything, but I've been thinking about moving back to the Midwest to be closer to them. Chicago's pretty close to Indiana, right?"

"Yes," I said this slowly, not entirely sure what he was saying.

He laughed. "No, Tina, I'm not saying moving in or anything like that. We both need our own space. But I've been looking at jobs in Indianapolis and Chicago. There's some interesting stuff going on up there in IT, even for an old guy like me." He paused. "Would you be upset if we were in the same town?"

Now it was my turn to laugh. "We are truly an odd couple, baby, to be asking ourselves that question. As long as I have my own place, it would be fun to be in the same city. I've missed you."

He exhaled. "Good, because I've actually been offered a job in Chicago."

I laughed again. "As long as it's not with the Stendahl Group, I think we're good."

44

Angela and Linda insisted on being my personal real estate advisors, dragging me to what felt like two dozen open houses. But it worked, and three weeks after Floyd Stendahl's co-op became a crime scene, I had an accepted offer on a large two-bedroom unit in the Edgewater Beach Apartments, the massive sunset pink Spanish Colonial co-op built as a sister to the original Edgewater Beach Hotel. It seemed appropriate, somehow.

Wrapping up Miami didn't take long. Charlie was civil enough when I stopped by to pick up the few personal items I had at the Mason Security office. Although it was an awkward few minutes, I wouldn't have felt right without saying goodbye in person. Despite how everything ended with the Stendahl assignment, the truth was Charlie had hired me, had given me a chance, when I hadn't had a lot of other options. I was grateful for that and told him so. He wished me the best, which felt as genuine as anything I'd heard him say. It was a good ending. As my mother always said, don't burn bridges if you don't have to.

I was packing up my soon-to-be-former apartment when the phone rang: Tom Donnelly. I hadn't spoken to Tom in the month since the paramedics had wheeled him away from Floyd's building. I wasn't sure what kind of conversation, if any, I wanted to have with him.

"Just calling to say hi," he said.

"How are you?"

"Up and about. Nearly back to normal."

"That's great. Back at work?" I asked.

"No. After all that, I just couldn't work for Bob anymore, so I'm retiring. Even after everything that happened, Bob's the same hard guy. He went back to the office to close a deal the day we buried his father. Unbelievable."

It was entirely believable to me, but I stayed silent.

"Did you hear the news about Stendahl Group?" Tom asked.

"I've been pretty focused on some other things, Tom. What news?"

"The State Department has started investigating Stendahl for selling restricted technology to the Russian government."

"Really? The State Department?"

"Yeah. Apparently, they're the ones who investigate ITAR. They came in a week ago and confiscated every hard drive in the downtown office. Because of the investigation, the City of Chicago's even backing away from Stendahl. Sounds like they'll probably lose the city contract."

"The State Department? Not the FBI?" I had assumed that the FBI's interest in the Stendahls had been because of the illegal sales.

"I guess." Tom sounded confused by my question. "At least, the people who came to the office were State Department."

Interesting. Did this mean that Stendahl was under federal scrutiny for something else? It reinforced my decision to stay in Chicago. My investigation wasn't over yet.

"Losing the city contract? That's pretty ironic, after everything—Krista, Stu, Bill. Terrance Jones. Adam Marek. The Russians."

"And Uncle Floyd."

I was quiet for a moment, digging deep to find compassion for Floyd Stendahl. I decided I could have sympathy for Tom without feeling sorry for the old man. "And Uncle Floyd," I finally agreed. "What's Bob say about all this?"

"He's fighting it, of course. He's got a full team of lawyers: defense attorneys, commercial litigators and politically connected guys. I'd say fifty-fifty that he gets away with it."

"He's gotten away with worse."

Tom didn't say anything for a minute. Then, finally: "Yeah, he has." Tom paused again. "Look, Tina, I wanted to thank you for what you did for me, and my family."

"I didn't do much, Tom. Whether I was there or not the cops would have showed up. You weren't going to die waiting another five minutes."

"But Suzi," he reminded me.

I smiled. "Okay, I'll take credit for that one." We both laughed. "How is Suzi?"

"Leaving Bob."

"Good for her. She needs to get a quick settlement, though, before the Feds finish with him."

"They actually had set up trusts in each of their names, and her attorney told her that the government can't get to hers. She'll be fine."

"Glad to hear it." Since the beginning of our call I'd been wondering whether to say something, and finally decided I should. "Tom, I'm moving to Chicago."

"Really?" His voice perked up.

"With my boyfriend." That was an exaggeration, possibly even a bit of a lie, but it helped set expectations. Tom Donnelly was a good-looking man and a nice guy, but there was no comparing him to Mark. Plus, the risk of seeing Bob Stendahl in social settings was more than I could stomach. Tom may have retired from the business, but they were still family.

"Oh." Dejected, but he recovered quickly. "Perhaps we can all get together for dinner sometime."

"Yes," I said. "Perhaps we can." And that wasn't a lie at all.

ACKNOWLEDGMENTS

For a variety of reasons, *Heavy Traffic* took over three years to write. As a result, there are many people who contributed to this story.

The inspiration for the story came from conversations with my friend Reppard, whose support buoyed me before and during a bumpy transition to life in Chicago.

It was my neighbor, John Kurtze, who suggested that Tina Johnson needed to live beyond *Passing Semis in the Rain*. John is a great developmental editor and our many cups of coffee at the Zanzibar Coffee Shop on Bryn Mawr Avenue fueled *Heavy Traffic*.

Another neighbor and friend, Gloria Gahagan, a longtime resident of Chicago's Edgewater neighborhood, provided wonderful descriptions of some of the settings in the story, particularly the Edgewater Beach Hotel. She and I also enjoyed more than a few coffees at Zanzibar.

Bernard C. Turner, a Chicago historian and author, was remarkably generous in providing a total stranger with background on the history of the Bronzeville neighborhood. I recommend his *A View of Bronzeville* for a short history of the people and buildings of Chicago's near South Side.

Author, activist, and community leader Chris Patterson helped me make sure some of the voices sounded authentic. My cousin Bill Epps shared his experience doing personal security from his military service. The Edgy Writers Group and in particular Sarz Maxwell provided developmental editing that was most valuable. The cover art was provided by the talented (and patient!) April Galamin. Eleanor York is a terrific editor.

Thank you to all of you for your gracious help. This is a better story because of you. Foibles and errors, however, are all my own.

ABOUT THE AUTHOR

Karen Goldner grew up in Omaha and spent the first half of her life in small Midwestern cities. After a six month break driving around the United States, she landed in Chicago, the greatest of all Midwestern cities. She spends her days working as a small business advisor and her evenings trying to balance political resistance, enjoying Chicago, and writing.

This is Karen's second Tina Johnson adventure, following *Passing Semis in the Rain*. She is also a contributor to *Over the Edge*, an anthology of short stories by the Edgy Writers Workshop, of which she is a member.

Made in the USA
Middletown, DE
22 January 2018